The
Riddle
of *Penncroft*
Farm

DOROTHEA JENSEN

The Riddle of Penncroft Farm

Gulliver Books
Harcourt, Inc.
San Diego   New York   London

Requests for permission to make copies of any part of the work should be
mailed to the following address: Permissions Department, Harcourt, Inc.,
6277 Sea Harbor Drive, Orlando, Florida 32887-6777.

The song "Geordie" is from One Hundred English Folk Songs © 1916
Theodore Presser Company. Reproduced by permission of the publisher.

www.harcourt.com

First Gulliver Books paperbacks edition 2001

Gulliver Books is a trademark of Harcourt, Inc., registered in the
United States of America and/or other jurisdictions.

Library of Congress Cataloging-in-Publication Data
Jensen, Dorothea.
The riddle of Penncroft Farm/Dorothea Jensen.
p. cm.—(Great Episodes)
Summary: Twelve-year-old Lars Olafson's move to his great-aunt's farm
near Valley Forge, Pennsylvania, brings him friendship with the ghost of
an eighteenth-century ancestor who recounts his adventures during the
American Revolution, helping Lars adjust to his new home and playing a
part in the search for a missing will.
1. Pennsylvania—History—Revolution, 1775–1783—Juvenile fiction.
[1. Pennsylvania—History—Revolution, 1775–1783—Fiction.
2. United States—History—Revolution, 1775–1783—Fiction.
3. Ghosts—Fiction. 4. Moving, Household—Fiction.
5. Great-aunts—Fiction. 6. Valley Forge (Pa.)—Fiction.]
I. Title. II. Series.
PZ7.J42997Ri 2001
[Fic]—dc21   2001016555
ISBN 0-15-216441-3

Text set in Fairfield MT Light
Display type set in Isadora and Imprint MT
Designed by Cathy Riggs

A C E G H F D B

To Nathaniel, Adam, Louisa,
and David

Special thanks to Arthur Bell, Janet Frankenfield,
Steve Gaskins, Maybelle Hettrick, William Iverson,
Martha Johnson, Elizabeth Keeton, Richard Pollak,
Jr., Elinor Williams, and Holly Windle.

The
Riddle
of Penncroft
Farm

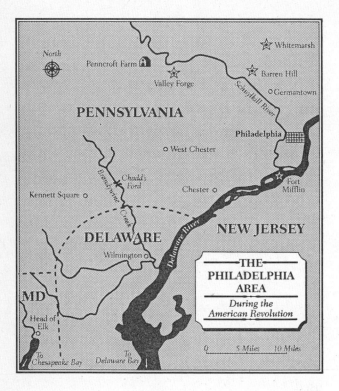

North

Penncroft Farm 🏠

Whitemarsh ✦

Barren Hill ✦

Valley Forge ✦

Germantown ○

Schuylkill River

PENNSYLVANIA

Philadelphia

West Chester ○

Brandywine Creek

Chadd's Ford

Chester ○

Fort Mifflin ✦

Kennett Square ○

DELAWARE

Delaware River

NEW JERSEY

Wilmington ○

MD

Head of Elk

To Chesapeake Bay

To Delaware Bay

—THE—
PHILADELPHIA
AREA

During the American Revolution

0   5 Miles   10 Miles

A Shade in the Window

"Penncroft Farm isn't *really* haunted, is it? You told me there are no such things as ghosts," I spluttered.

"Well, if it makes you feel any better, Lars, I swear that *I* never saw anything supernatural there," my mother replied. "It was George who swore the place was loaded with ghosts. But then, my brother always did love to tell tall tales."

Mom was sitting in the front seat of our car and I was stuck in the back as usual, so I couldn't see her face. But I could guess her expression from the sound of her voice. It had the sad tone she always used to talk about Uncle George.

"I wish you wouldn't mention ghosts, Sandra," Dad protested. "Penncroft can be a *very* spooky spot when the wind moans through that old orchard at night. And you know the house was built

before the American Revolution. I'll bet a lot's happened there."

"I suppose George Washington slept there," I
scoffed.

"No, I'm afraid not, honey," Mom said, "much to
Aunt Cass's eternal regret. Of course, he did spend a
winter at Valley Forge, which is only a stone's throw
away."

I leaned forward eagerly. "Valley Forge? Is that
an amusement park like Valley Fair back home?"

"Lars! Don't tell me you've never heard of Valley Forge! Didn't you study the Revolutionary War
in school?" Mom exclaimed.

"Give me a break! We've been doing Minnesota
history—you know, explorers like Zebulon Pike.
Geez, I hope I don't have to learn a bunch of stuff
about Pennsylvania. It's not fair having to learn two
state histories just because I have to move."

Dad humphed. "You'll change your mind when
we get into Philadelphia and see the Liberty Bell
and Independence Hall. Too bad we don't have
time today."

"Don't care if I ever see 'em," I muttered.

"He's still upset about moving, Erik," said Mom.

Dad's voice deepened. "I know it's tough, but

he'll get over it once he makes some new friends and meets your aunt Cass."

Mom twisted around to look at me, although it was getting too dark to see much of anything. "When George and I spent summers at Penncroft Farm, he used to play tricks on Aunt Cass. Cass called it *bamboozling*—that's one of her favorite words. It means fooling someone."

"What did she do to get back at him?" I asked.

Mom chuckled. "Among other things, she apple-pied his bed. That's the old-fashioned name for short sheeting—probably comes from folding the sheet in a triangle like a piece of pie."

"Like Peter used to do to me?" I thought of how my older brother folded my sheets and tucked them tight so I couldn't get into bed. That reminded me that Peter got to stay in Minnesota because he was in college.

"I'll bet *you* were the best bamboozler, Sandra," Dad teased.

"Not me! I had better things to do. But Lars, you bamboozled Aunt Cass thoroughly the last time we came, even though you were only two. Whenever she'd go out to hang up the wash, you'd pull in all the latchstrings and strand her outside."

"I did not! I don't even know what latchstrings are!"

Dad explained that a latchstring was a cord that could be pulled through a hole in a door to open it from the outside.

"Cass is crazy about kids who get into mischief, especially ones named George, like my brother and you," Mom said. "Even though George is only your middle name, it still works like a charm on Aunt Cass. Guess it reminds her of our ancestor named George. Apparently he was really something."

"Anyway, Lars *George* Olafson, don't be surprised if Aunt Cass bamboozles *you*. She owes you a couple after that latchstring business," Dad warned.

Trading practical jokes with an old lady didn't sound too exciting. I stared out the car window at the full moon lighting up the empty fields, and a wave of loneliness shivered through me. "Boy, you weren't kidding when you said this place was out in the country," I said.

Dad replied, "Yeah, and it's easy to get lost out here. Instead of coming to nice, square corners like in the Midwest, these little country roads snake all over the place. And they've got screwy names, like *Seek-No-Further Pike*."

I perked up at the mention of pike. Catching

walleyed and northern pike was my specialty. So were puns. "Seek-No-Further Pike? Is that what they called Zebulon when he retired from exploring, or does it mean the fishing season's over?"

My double pun got double the usual groan from my parents.

"*Seek-no-further* was the name of an apple grown around here a couple of centuries ago," Mom explained.

"And it's *pike* as in *turnpike*, Lars. Seek-No-Further Pike is the road that goes past Penncroft Farm," Dad went on. "It runs all the way to Valley Forge. By the way, Cass says there are bike paths and picnic places up there now. Seems ironic to go to Valley Forge for fun, though."

"I wonder if our ancestor George was there," Mom mused.

"Oh, *him* again," I muttered. I couldn't have cared less about some moldy old ancestor. The next subject, however, did grab my attention; I hunched forward to hear every word.

"Did you call the school yet, Erik?"

"Uh-huh. Lars is lucking out. There's a teachers' convention tomorrow, so he doesn't have to start until Friday."

It didn't sound like lucking out to me. I'd

counted on the weekend at least before plunging in at a strange school. Besides, this weekend was Halloween. I hated to think about my friends back in Minneapolis trick-or-treating around our neighborhood without me. Actually, I quit wearing a costume years ago because I felt so dumb in one. But my friend Pat dressed up, and I'd go with him and wait on the sidewalk. Good old Patrick—he'd always share his hauls with me.

"Hey, wait a minute! Where will I go trick-or-treating on Halloween?" I asked. "It's this Saturday."

"Sorry, honey, I guess you won't get to go this year. There aren't any neighbors close enough to walk to—at least at night," Mom said. "But don't worry, we'll have our own old-fashioned Halloween party."

"Great." I slouched back in the seat and closed my eyes. The sound of my parents' voices seemed to come from far away.

"Have you had a chance to ask Aunt Cass about her will, Erik?" my mother asked anxiously.

"Not really, honey. It's pretty awkward. I thought maybe it would be better if *you* asked her."

"It makes me feel like such a vulture, but we do have to be practical. After all, Cass is ninety years old."

Dad put the car into low gear for a hilly curve. "I can't believe she would urge us to pull up stakes and make Penncroft our home unless she planned to let us stay after she's gone. Surely she's changed her will so we inherit the farm, Sandra. It's too bad you said you didn't want the place when she first asked you, after George died."

"Yes, but back then we didn't think we'd ever move here. Then Cass wrote that she was leaving the farm to be used for a museum of the First American Civil War, whatever that means."

"Well, she did say that the museum idea wasn't working out."

"We'll have to ask her about her will sometime. Really, if she'd rather have Penncroft be a museum, that's fine, too. I'll be happy wherever we live, Erik, but I *would* hate to uproot Lars again. Moving's been awfully hard on him. Still, I'm glad this Philadelphia job came along so you don't have to travel anymore. Oh! There's the covered bridge!" Mom said excitedly.

Rattling through the old wooden structure roused me. "I've never been in one of these before," I said. "It's pretty neat."

"It is quaint," Mom said. "But that's not the only quaint thing around. Wait until you see your bed—the one my brother used to sleep in at Penncroft. It has a canopy."

"A can o' pee? You mean this place doesn't have bathrooms?"

Mom shook her finger at me. "You know very well what I mean, Lars. A canopy *over* the bed, not under it!"

"It better not have ruffles," I protested.

"Oh, don't worry," she said. "As canopies go, it's not a bit frilly. It was masculine enough for your ancestor George to sleep under. Besides, George himself is hanging in your room. So's his wife."

"H-h-h-hanging . . . ," I stuttered, every horror movie I'd ever seen replaying before my eyes.

"She's only teasing you, Lars," Dad said. "It's a portrait of the old boy by Charles Willson Peale, who painted most of the Revolution big shots, like Washington and Franklin. Well, here we are!"

The headlights picked out a crooked wooden fence and a post with a sign in spiky, old-fashioned letters. "'Penncroft Farm,'" I read out loud. "'Established 1760.'"

Dad eased the car around the corner and started up the driveway. "Don't even think of skateboarding down this, Lars," he said. "There's quite a drop-off on the other side of the pike. You'd break a leg if you went off it, and maybe your neck."

"It's too rutted for skateboarding anyway, Dad," I replied. Then, as we jounced up the long, steep driveway, I stuck my head out the window to check out my new home.

Even by moonlight I could tell that it was different from any house I'd ever seen. It looked as if someone hadn't been able to decide what sort of house he wanted, so he'd hooked several kinds together. There were dark, bumpy stones on the middle part, but the left section was shingled like our old Minnesota house; the right was covered with white stuff.

Mom said the pointy windows were called eyebrow windows.

"Okay, then, so which window belongs to the room where the ghost hangs out?" I asked, only half in jest.

"Now *that* is something you're going to have to discover for yourself," she said, giving her version of a fiendish laugh.

I winced. "Aw, Mom, cut it out. You don't honestly think you scared me with that dumb story about ghosts."

"I didn't mean to *scare* you, honey. These ghosts are *very* friendly; nothing to fret about at all, according to George. What an imagination that brother of mine had, and what a tease he was!" She sighed.

"That's where your room is, Lars," Dad said. "The far left window on the second floor—the one with the light on."

I glanced up. Someone was silhouetted in the window of what was to be my room. Whoever it was slowly raised one hand. It reminded me of the picture sent on the *Pioneer 10* space probe to greet the rest of the universe. "Is that Aunt Cass waving at us?" I asked.

"I don't see her," Mom said. "Where is she?"

"There—in my room," I said impatiently.

"You must be seeing things, Lars," Dad responded. "Cass hardly ever goes up there now. The stairs are getting to be too much for her."

"Maybe it's a window shade flapping in the breeze," Mom said.

"B-but can't you see..." I looked up again, but the figure was gone.

The headlights swooped past the front of an old barn as we pulled to a stop behind the house. As soon as I climbed out of the car, I started toward the back door. I wanted to know who had been looking out of that window.

But before I'd taken more than a few steps, an eerie sound stopped me in my tracks. A spooky stream of notes, wheezy and piercing, was coming from the house.

"What's *that*?" I said in a hoarse whisper.

Without missing a beat, Mom answered matter-of-factly, "Bach's Toccata and Fugue in D Minor, unless I miss my guess."

Dad sang along. "Duddle-la...deedle deedle deet deeeeee. Remember, Lars, when we saw *20,000 Leagues Under the Sea*? That's the pipe organ piece Captain Nemo played on board his submarine."

"Oh yeah," I gulped. "Captain Nemo on the *Nautilus*."

"It's only Cass playing her pump organ," Mom said. "Go in and introduce yourself, Lars. You're the one she's most anxious to see. Besides, I have a surprise for her I have to dig out."

Suddenly I wasn't too keen about walking into that creepy old place by myself. Swallowing hard, I marched to the door and tried the handle. It didn't budge.

Dad came up and set down a couple of suit-cases. "Darn, she's pulled in the latchstring. She'll never hear the knocker over the sound of that organ. Run around to the front door, Lars, and see if that string's out. Just give it a pull." He headed back to the car, where Mom was rummaging through the trunk.

I trudged around to the front door and tugged on the leather thong hanging out beneath the door handle. Slowly, slowly, the old wooden door creaked open.

Inside, candlelight flickered from a candelabra on a pump organ that did look like Captain Nemo's. My great-aunt sat playing at the keyboard, her feet vigorously working the pedals below. I crossed over and timidly touched her on the shoulder. Startled, she shrieked so loudly that I echoed a pretty re-spectable squawk myself.

Aunt Cass ratcheted herself around on the organ bench, and I got a good look at her. Except for the color of her face, she looked exactly like the witch in *The Wizard of Oz*. I noticed her hand was over her heart as if she planned to say the pledge of allegiance, but she exclaimed, "My, but you took me by surprise, young man. I presume you *are* George?"

"Why, n-no—my name's Lars," I stammered.

She waved away my words. "Yes, yes, of course, but I prefer to call you L. George—George for short."

Not knowing what else to say, I asked if I could try the organ.

She nodded. "You'll find it's better exercise than any newfangled Nautilus machine," she said, pursing her lips.

I wondered if Captain Nemo would agree.

Just then my mother came running in, looking alarmed and sounding breathless. "What was all that screaming?" she asked.

"We took each other aback," Aunt Cass said. "A good beginning. This George promises to be as much fun as your brother. Now, give me a good hug, Sandra. It's about time you came back to Penncroft Farm!"

While they were hugging, Dad came in loaded with luggage. "Here's what you were looking for, Sandra," he said, handing her a wrapped box.

Mom took the package and gave it to Aunt Cass. "I've been meaning to give you this for a long time."

"You shouldn't waste your money on me," my great-aunt declared.

Mom shook her head slowly. "I didn't."

Aunt Cass unwrapped the package. Inside was a wooden toy—a sort of cup on a stick with a ball connected to it by a leather cord. She stared at it without saying a word, then deftly flipped the ball into the cup. "I don't understand," she said, turning to gaze at Mom. "Why did you bring this to me?"

"When George..." Mom's voice choked up. She cleared her throat and went on. "After George was killed in Vietnam, all his personal effects were sent to me. This old cup and ball came with his other stuff."

"But why didn't you give it to one of your boys, Sandra?"

"Because I remembered you didn't just give it to George. He had to *earn* it in that historical treasure hunt of yours."

Aunt Cass's face wrinkled into a smile. "Yes, that was quite a challenge for George, but he finally figured out the hiding place on his own. All it took was the right spirit."

"That's all *he'd* ever say, the rat; he was so smug about keeping it secret! After that I never could find him when we played hide-and-seek. It must have been a great hiding place."

"Yes, indeed," Aunt Cass said softly.

14

"I don't suppose you'd tell me where it is, would you?" asked my mother hopefully.

"I've never *told* anybody, Sandra. It has to be discovered, you know. Just like your brother did," Aunt Cass replied, an unreadable look on her face.

There was nothing unreadable about Mom's expression—her disappointment was obvious. "Well, anyway, I've brought your toy back where it belongs, Cass," she said, and went out.

Aunt Cass flipped the ball into the cup two more times. Itching to try it, I stretched out my hand without thinking.

My father must have noticed. "Maybe there's someone else here who might like a chance to 'earn' the thing," he said.

Aunt Cass's faded blue eyes studied me intently. "I have only one thing to say to you, George," she said, then paused. I guess I expected her to say something about my doing a treasure hunt like Uncle George. Instead, she frowned and sternly asked, "Why didn't you pick more peas?"

There was a kind of strangled choke of laughter from Dad, but he only asked if Aunt Cass had been upstairs looking out the window. "Lars thought he saw you waving from his bedroom window as we drove in," he said, sounding amused.

"Oh, he did, did he?" Aunt Cass raised one eyebrow and gave me a funny look, as if she were trying to guess what size I wore or something. Then she turned back to Dad. "Now Erik, you know I seldom go up these stairs anymore."

"That's what I told him. He must be so sleepy he's seeing things. C'mon, Lars, I'll show you the way to bed," Dad said.

I was too tired to argue. Silently I followed him up the narrow staircase and down the dark hallway to my room. I went straight to the window. A shade fluttered a little in the breeze, but there was nothing faintly resembling the guy on the *Pioneer 10* picture.

Dad joined me at the window. "You must have seen the curtains blowing behind the shade," he said. He pulled down the sash. "Can't leave this open—it'll probably get pretty cold tonight. After all, it's almost Halloween. Now, hop into bed as fast as you can, Lars. See you in the morning."

"Wait a minute, Dad. Why did Aunt Cass ask me about picking peas? Does she have all her marbles?" I asked.

"Every one," Dad chuckled. "She was referring to the last time we were here. She had a bumper crop of peas in her garden and sent you and Peter out there with big buckets to pick some. Peter kept at it, but you came back in a couple of minutes— with only two peas in your bucket. She couldn't understand why anybody would let little things like heat, bugs, or a *very* wet diaper get in the way of pea picking."

"I'll pick peas for her now if she likes," I offered nobly, "just as long as I don't have to eat any." There was nothing I hated more than peas.

"I'm sure she'll be happy to hear that. Good night, Lars," Dad said, and went out.

Quickly I got ready for bed. As I climbed under the canopy, I glanced up, remembering my can o' pee pun. With a smirk, I started to slide under the covers. But my feet made it only partway down, stranding my knees somewhere in the vicinity of my chin.

I'd been bamboozled by Aunt Cass.

2

Downward Ho the Wagon

I woke up with jumbled covers and cold toes. For a minute I couldn't remember where I was, then it all came flooding back: Pennsylvania, Penncroft Farm, Aunt Cass, and the apple-pied bed.

Pulling the blankets around me, I leaned out from under the canopy to look for the pictures Mom had mentioned, but found only one—a painting of a man about my dad's age. The picture was almost entirely black and white, from the guy's short, dark hair and black coat to the snowy ruffles of his shirt. The only color on the canvas was the bright blue of his eyes, which seemed to be gazing solemnly at me. Trailing covers, I crossed to read the metal plate on the painting: *George Hargreaves, Painted by Charles Willson Peale, Philadelphia, 1805.*

Suddenly, the unmistakable scent of frying bacon wafted up to my nose. Hurrying into my clothes, I went down the stairs two at a time, then stopped at the kitchen door to look around.

An enormous stone fireplace, deep and high enough for me and several friends (if I'd had any) to stand up in, covered one wall. A big copper kettle swung from a long black rod, and there were metal objects on the hearth that looked like something from a torture chamber. A wooden bench with a tall back stuck out from each side of the fireplace.

At the other end of the kitchen, Dad sat at the table, reading the paper. Mom was manning the toaster while Aunt Cass fried eggs and bacon at a modern stove.

When I heard Mom ask who Aunt Cass was playing tricks on these days, it sounded like my cue, so I cleared my throat loudly from the doorway. Both women jumped, and Aunt Cass repeated that pledge of allegiance business with her hand to her heart.

They both said good morning, then Mom turned back to her aunt. "Speaking of tricks, Cass, I told Lars that instead of trick-or-treating, we'd have an old-fashioned Halloween party here. Could we cook in the old fireplace? Maybe mull cider in the old copper kettle and pop corn like we used to? Maybe invite some friends?"

Aunt Cass took a deep breath and straightened up. "Of course, Sandra," she said briskly. "I'll call Judge Bank."

She slipped the eggs out of the frying pan onto the plates, Mom passed the toast and nudged Dad out of his newspaper, and we all began to eat. From across the table, my great-aunt gazed at me as soberly as the guy in the picture upstairs, but the way her lips twitched wasn't solemn at all.

"So, George," she said, "how did you sleep?"

"No problem," I replied, squelching a smile, "once I got used to the *short* bed. Then it was easy as apple pie."

Dad spoke up, something he seldom does before finishing his first cup of coffee. "These antique beds are a little short for me, too, Cass. Guess I'll have to set up our king-size bed."

"If you think *these* beds are short, you should see the one George Washington slept in at Valley Forge," Mom put in. "It's only about five feet long, and he was over six feet tall. I've never understood how he did it."

"The beds were shorter in those days because people slept propped up on pillows. They believed it prevented tuberculosis," Aunt Cass explained. "The notion probably started because sitting up eased their breathing when they *did* get a lung disease."

"Even if Washington slept sitting up, I bet he wasn't very comfy on that short bed at Valley Forge," Mom retorted. "Gee, Lars, I can hardly wait to show you his headquarters up there!"

"The main Valley Forge museum is interesting, too," Aunt Cass said with a sniff. "Although I don't feel that it tells the whole story. Not everybody around here supported the Revolution, you know. It was really a civil war—the first American civil war."

Mom glanced at Dad and nervously crumbled her toast into her saucer. "Um . . . Aunt Cass . . . I've been meaning to ask you about that museum idea of yours. You mean a kind of portrait gallery or something, with that pair of Peale paintings upstairs?"

"Only half a pair, actually," I said, my mouth full of egg.

Mom's eyes opened wider. "Aunt Cass," she sputtered, "you didn't sell one of the family portraits, did you?"

"Simmer down, Sandra. Of course I didn't sell it—I gave it to the Hargreaveses. They're descendants of George and his wife and have just as much right to the portrait as we do."

"You mean Will Hargreaves? Is he still around?"

"Next farm over," replied Aunt Cass.

"The one called Blackberry Hill Farm?" asked Dad. "That's a beautiful old place. Didn't know any Hargreaveses lived there."

"A Hargreaves son married into the family over there around the time of the Civil War. That makes Will a distant cousin."

"He and George used to pal around," Mom chimed in. "Oh, Aunt Cass, remember when the two of them went through that hippie phase? They were so disappointed when you *liked* their ponytails!"

Dad stood up. "Well, I've got to go. Don't unpack everything today, honey. We've got lots of time to settle in," he said.

Aunt Cass nodded. "He's right, Sandra. The boxes can wait."

Mom went over to Dad. "Okay, we won't go into a frenzy. But I am going to get our bedroom set to rights, so *you* don't have to sleep sitting up. And Lars, I don't expect apple-pie order in your room right away, but at least make the bed."

"Right," I said, sneaking a look at Aunt Cass, who was sneaking an amused look back.

After Mom and Dad went out, Aunt Cass slapped her hands down on the table. "Now then, how would you like a tour of your new home?" she asked.

"Okay," I said, mostly to be polite.

"Help me clean up and afterward I'll show you around."

I cleared and wiped the table, then swept the plank floor while Aunt Cass did the dishes. Then she picked up a sweater and put it on. "Better wear your jacket," she said. "Sandra put it in one of the settles last night."

"Huh?"

"The settles—those high-backed benches. The seats open up. That's where I keep hats and mittens and things."

I flipped open one of the wooden benches. My jacket was inside. "It looks like my coat is already settled in," I punned.

"You're a punster— good," remarked Aunt Cass without a glimmer of a smile. "Always liked puns; never much good at making 'em up. Come on." She pushed open the door and we went outside.

As I shut the door behind me, I touched the

leather thong hanging underneath the handle. "So that's a latchstring," I said, innocently.

Aunt Cass shook her finger at me, then said, "Now then, George, we'll go to the orchard first. That used to be the heart of the farm. Of course, the fruit trees are dead now, more's the pity."

We walked up past the barn and the pond that lay beyond it. Aunt Cass pointed out two sycamore trees at the pond's edge that were planted to mark the location of drinkable water in colonial times.

"Ah," I said, pretending more interest than I felt.

She glanced at me, then moved through a rickety gate in the zigzag rail fence.

"Don't try climbing this fence until your dad has a chance to see if it's safe. I'm afraid I've let it go since I have no more animals to keep in. No sheep in the meadow or cows in the corn," she said. "Here's the orchard. It doesn't look like much now, but generations back it was a working orchard with more than a thousand fruit trees—apples and pears and peaches."

"Are these Seek-no-further apple trees?" I asked.

Aunt Cass sighed. "No, those all died and were chopped up for firewood years ago."

I climbed one of the sturdier-looking trees and looked around. "Hey, somebody's riding a horse over there," I said.

"That's probably Pat Hargreaves."

"You mean there's a kid living so close?" I exclaimed. "Named Pat? My best friend in Minneapolis is named Patrick!"

"Wouldn't it be nice to become best friends with a Pat here, then?" Aunt Cass said, her face crinkling in an impish smile. "And this Pat's a particular favorite of mine. Goes to the same school you will, probably in your class. And crazy about horses—practically lives in the saddle. Do you ride?"

"Only a couple of times at camp. I fell off once when the saddle slid under the horse's belly."

"Maybe you could get Pat to teach you how to ride." She peered up at me. "I hope the two of you will get along. Pat's terrific—helps me out around Penncroft Farm. I don't know what I'd do without— George! What are you doing up there! Be care—!"

I jumped out of the tree before my great-aunt could finish her sentence. Her affection for Pat Hargreaves made me a little jealous. I half hoped he wouldn't turn up in my class.

"I imagine you'll meet the Hargreaveses at meeting on Sunday," Aunt Cass said. "They're Friends, too."

"I thought they were relations," I said, brushing pieces of bark off my jeans.

"I mean they belong to the Society of Friends. It's our religion, Lars. We're pacifists—we don't believe in war. Some people call us Quakers."

"I thought you meant the Hargreaveses were *amigos*."

"As a matter of fact, they're *amigos,* too," she said, smiling. She took my arm, and we started back toward the barn.

I looked at the distant rider again. "There's something else I don't get. If the Hargreaveses are descendants of our ancestors who owned Penncroft Farm, why didn't *they* end up with it?"

Aunt Cass gave me an approving look. "I like honesty in a man," she said, "and honesty in a woman, for that matter. So I'll tell you straight. It's always been a family tradition to leave Penncroft Farm to the member of the next generation who has a little something extra, a sort of feeling about the place—I guess you could call it being a kindred spirit. Your uncle George was the one in your mother's generation and he . . . well, you know what happened to him.

"Now, Pat is a kindred spirit, but also an only child who will inherit Blackberry Hill Farm. That's why, when your mother told me years ago that she wasn't interested in moving here, I thought to leave Penncroft Farm for a museum. And this is one of the things to be exhibited."

She pointed to an old wagon, parked under a kind of lean-to attached to the barn. The barn was built into the side of the hill, and a fairly stiff slope ran down to the driveway below. I wondered how they had gotten the wagon up there.

"This wagon dates back to the American Revolution," Aunt Cass said, giving the wheel a little thump with her hand. She gave me another of those measuring looks.

I didn't care how old the thing was, but it occurred to me that if I couldn't ride on top of a horse with style, maybe I could learn to drive one. "Have you got a horse to pull it, Aunt Cass?" I asked eagerly.

"Afraid not, but we do have some harness, and Pat keeps the wagon in pretty good repair. Maybe now that you're living here, we can buy a horse to get the old rig moving again. That is, if you'll learn from Pat how to hitch up and drive it properly."

"Pat Hargreaves seems to be an expert on everything," I said, more or less to myself.

My muttering didn't get past Aunt Cass. "No, not quite everything," she said, patting my hand. "But remember: Pat grew up in the country and you're a city boy. Things are a bit different out here."

"You can say that again." I climbed up on the wagon and sat down on the seat. Underneath was a lever. I grabbed it and pretended to shift gears. I guess I thought it was too rotten or rusty to do anything. I was wrong. The lever moved easily in my hand and the wagon started to roll.

"Look out!" I shouted at Aunt Cass, who stepped backward in the nick of time, only to lose her balance and fall to the ground. I looked back to where she lay, too worried about her to think about what was happening to me. Then, as the wagon rolled past the house, I caught a glimpse of Mom at the window. The look on her face scared me. As the wagon lurched down the steep, rutted drive, picking up speed with every passing second, I tried to get up the nerve to jump off, but the sight of the ground rushing by kept my hands riveted to the wagon seat. With rising panic, I fixed my eyes on the pike below and the bone-breaking drop-off I knew was beyond it. In my mind I could see myself flying through the air and hear the splintering of wood. Then, suddenly, just before the wagon hurtled across the road to plunge over the edge, somebody reached out and pulled hard on the lever. The wagon groaned to a stop.

For a moment I sat there, hearing nothing but my own gasps and the faint creak of the Penncroft sign. Then, once I caught my breath, I started to think. Somebody had pulled that lever. That somebody had not been me. I whirled around on the seat to see who was behind me. There were some iron tools, some leather straps, and a rusty old pulley. No one was on the wagon but me.

I stared down at my own hand; except for the bitten-off fingernails, it didn't look like the one I'd seen grip the lever. Dazed, I peered around. Had I imagined the whole thing?

My mother's voice broke into my confusion. "Lars, are you all right? Answer me! Lars!" She sounded pretty hysterical.

"I'm fine, Mom," I shouted back, my voice a bit shaky.

She came running down. "How did you stop that thing?"

"I didn't. There was . . . that is . . . didn't you see anybody in here with me?" I quavered.

"Honestly, Lars! This is no time to be fooling around. Where's Aunt Cass?"

I suddenly remembered where I'd left Aunt Cass. "Oh, Mom, she fell! Up there!" I jumped down from the seat and sprinted up the hill. Aunt Cass was sitting helplessly in the middle of the gravel driveway, her hands over her face. When I squatted down next to her, I saw that she was shaking all over.

Mom knelt down. "Are you all right?" she asked anxiously.

My great-aunt dropped her hands, and we could see how helpless she was—helpless with laughter.

Seeing that she was all right, I blurted out, "Aunt Cass, did *you* see anybody on the wagon with me? I saw this hand pull the lever and . . ."

"Panic can do strange things to your perceptions, honey," Mom said soothingly as she helped Aunt Cass to her feet. "I saw you go by, Lars. You were the only one in that dreadful wagon."

Aunt Cass stared at me, then nodded emphatically. "George, I think you've been *properly* introduced to Penncroft Farm now!"

Mom put an arm around each of us and said, in an obvious attempt to change the subject, "Let's go eat some of Cass's pasties—good old colonial meat pies."

"And we'll wash down the pasties with some ice-cold squash!" Aunt Cass said, giving Mom a wink.

"Wash it down with ice-cold squash?" I squeaked. "That sounds disgusting!" I hated squash almost as much as peas.

"Relax," Mom laughed. "Squash is a kind of punch made of orange juice and lemonade, or the juice from some other squashed fruit. The Founding Fathers were all big squash fans."

I don't know if it was my close call on the wagon or the thought of drinkable squash, but suddenly I felt a little dizzy.

"Toto," I said under my breath, "I don't think we're in Minnesota anymore."

3

A Custom
of Costumes

The next day I woke up feeling groggy. I had stared up at my canopy for hours thinking about the hand that had clutched the brake. It was not my hand. It couldn't have been.

Mom knocked on my door to get me up for school, and there was no time to wonder about the day before. She hustled me along and all too soon we were pulling up in front of my new school.

"Look how big the school grounds are," Mom said in an encouraging tone of voice. "And did you see the obstacle course? I'll bet you'll like going through that."

I gave her a scornful look.

We went in, registered, and in what seemed like only a millisecond, stood reading the sign on my new classroom.

"'Mrs. Hettrick. Grade Six.' Guess this is it, Lars. Want me to come in with you?" Mom whispered.

"No, thanks," I replied, trying to sound brave.

Mom gave me an anxious look. "All right, then, I guess I'll run along." She took a couple of steps, then came back again. "Do you remember which bus to take and where to get off?"

Fear was making me irritable. "Yes, yes! Bus number eight, and I get off on Seek-No-Further Pike. How could I ever forget *that* name?" I snapped.

"Okay. Bye, honey," Mom said uncertainly, and finally left.

With a sinking feeling, I watched her walk away. Taking a deep breath, I turned the handle and walked through the door to meet my new class-mates. I couldn't believe my eyes. I'd expected Pennsylvania kids might look different from my Minnesota friends, but not *this* different. Open-mouthed, I stared at a room full of punks and pirates, ghosts and Martians. I had forgotten it was nearly Halloween.

A woman dressed like Raggedy Ann came up to me. "You must be our new student," she said with a warm smile, trying to smooth orange yarn hair out of her eyes. "I'm Mrs. Hettrick. Welcome to the

33

class. Oh, and Happy Halloween!" She glanced at my jeans and sweatshirt with dismay. "But you don't have a costume on! What a shame you didn't know we were having a party. Well, it doesn't matter. Come meet the other students."

A group of kids had gathered around and were looking curiously at me. Embarrassed, I blabbed out the first thing that came into my head. "Where I come from, only *kindergartners* wear costumes to school."

Several girls nudged each other and whispered. One tall, sandy-haired girl in a pirate costume was edging up, but stopped when she heard me. Her smile vanished.

Who cares about girls, anyway? I said to myself.

"Where are you from?" one of the girls asked.

"Minneapolis, Minnesota," I said. My lips felt a little numb and stiff, as if I'd just had a filling.

A short, fat kid in a cowboy outfit laughed. It was not a friendly laugh. "Minneapolis—that hick town! My dad says that's in flyover country."

The pirate girl looked at me with sympathetic brown eyes—or eye, actually, since an eye patch covered one of them. "Oh, Eddie, don't be such a jerk," she said to the cowboy.

Mrs. Hettrick raised her hand for silence. "We're going to take a little break from our party so that everyone can meet our new student. Take your regular seats, so he can tell us something about himself."

Grumbling, the other kids walked into the next room and sat down. Thinking I had already said more than enough, I followed the teacher to the front of the room.

"Um, I just moved here from Minneapolis," I said, then stopped. I couldn't think of anything else to say.

"Do you have any brothers or sisters?" Mrs. Hettrick prompted.

"Uh-huh," I said, feeling dumber by the second.

"Well, which do you have, brothers or sisters?"

"Brothers ... or rather, *one* brother. *He* gets to stay in Minnesota."

"Flyover country," somebody whispered from the back row.

Mrs. Hettrick asked me to introduce myself.

"Lars ... Lars Olafson. It's a Norwegian name," I added.

The same someone snickered in the back row and called out, "It's Nor*weird*gian." It was the chubby kid in the cowboy suit that the pirate girl had called Eddie—and a jerk.

"Edward Owens...," Mrs. Hettrick started to say, but the kid interrupted her.

"Edward Owens the Tenth," he said, putting his stubby nose a little higher in the air.

She frowned. "Edward Whatever-you-are, either you stop being rude or you'll spend the rest of our party parked in the office."

Her threat brought a ripple of applause from the rest of the class. It made me feel a little better to know that the other kids weren't too crazy about Eddie.

The applause got louder when Mrs. Hettrick told the class they could go back to their party. Most of the kids returned to the open area where the games were set up. I stayed where I was.

Mrs. Hettrick took me aside. "I hope you'll have no objection to wearing a costume on Colonial Day," she said.

"Colonial Day? What's that?"

"It's a special event we have every year—the big finish of our unit on colonial life and the American Revolution. We have crafts and food and games from that era, and this year Pat Hargreaves is going to provide some authentic music."

I looked around at the other students. So my distant cousin, Aunt Cass's favorite kid, *was* in my class. Where was this wonderful boy, anyway? And if he was so wonderful, why hadn't he spoken up when that Eddie creep was making fun of me?

The girl pirate, who had stuck around, was chattering about Colonial Day. "We've been getting ready all fall," she said enthusiastically, "researching customs back to the early settlements in Pennsylvania—William Penn and everybody—and my mom's making me a long skirt like Martha Washington's, and—"

"B-but *I* don't know anything about William Penn or...anybody," I broke in. "All I've been studying this year is Minnesota history, starting way back in 1830 with—"

"Eighteen-thirty!" somebody said sarcastically. That guy Eddie again. "That's all? Pennsylvania was settled way before that—in 1682. And *my* great-great-great-great-great—well, at least *seven* greats—grandfather was one of the first guys to come over."

Mrs. Hettrick looked as if she'd heard all of this before. "Yes, Eddie, we know about your illustrious ancestors," she said frostily, "but right now I have to talk to Lars about catching up with the rest of the class." She turned to me. "Don't worry—I'll give you some books to read, and maybe you can write a special report instead of taking the tests."

"That's not fair," Eddie whined.

"I'm sure Lars had to take just as many tests back in Minneapolis as we've had here, Eddie. Why should he be penalized because he had to move during the school year? Now, *that* wouldn't be fair." She went over to her desk.

I glanced at Eddie and thought that just moving into a classroom with a jerk like him was penalty enough.

The girl pirate sat down at the desk next to me. "Aunt Cass told me you were coming, but she called you George, so I wasn't sure if you were the guy she meant," she said, putting up her eye patch. "I guess we're distant cousins or something. My name's Pat."

"*You're* Pat Hargreaves? But you're a *girl!*"

Pat reached for a chain at her neck and toyed nervously with the ring that hung on it. "Well, yes, I—," she started to say.

"That's all I need. My only neighbor is a *girl!*" I muttered. I guess I muttered louder than usual, because she gave me a hurt look, got up, and walked away. I felt bad, but after all, it wasn't my fault Aunt Cass had bamboozled me again.

Someone else sat down by me—the cowboy, unfortunately.

"If you live anywhere near Patty Hargreaves, you must still be a hick. She's really out in the boondocks," he said.

"Yeah," I replied, clenching my fist in an effort to keep my temper. "We live at a place called Penncroft Farm..."

Eddie jumped up so fast his cowboy hat fell off. "You've moved to *Penncroft Farm*? Just wait until I tell my dad!" he shouted. I wondered if he were crazy or something.

Mrs. Hettrick came back with an armload of books. "Eddie," she said sternly, "one more outburst from you and *I'll* have to tell your father a thing or two. Here, Lars, this should get you started." She handed me the stack of books.

Eddie picked up his hat and left, but as he walked off he whispered, "Just wait till my dad finds out."

I picked up one of the books Mrs. Hettrick had given me, opened it at random, and stared blindly at the page.

The rest of the day dragged by. I was so embarrassed by the stupid things I'd said and so angry at the teasing I'd received that I didn't speak to anyone.

When the bell finally rang, I followed the others out to the circular drive where the buses were lined up. I found the number eight bus and walked stiffly to the backseat. It appeared that I lived the farthest away from school because almost everyone got off the bus before I did. Only Pat Hargreaves remained, sitting up in front near the driver. I hoped she'd forgotten what I'd said to her, but the look she gave me as she climbed down from the bus said plainly she remembered it all.

It was only a little farther to my stop, and, with a sigh of relief, I jumped down from the bus. *No school until Monday,* I thought happily as I started down the pike. There was still a half-mile walk to Penncroft Farm, but I dawdled along. I was in no great hurry to get home to Mom's questions about my first day at school. Besides, it was a really nice day, and I didn't want to waste it unpacking cartons.

I gave a tentative kick to a good-size stone on the shoulder of the road. It skittered nicely across the blacktop, so I kicked it down the narrow, winding road. I was so intent on what I was doing that I didn't pay attention to anything else. I suppose that's why, when I came to the old covered bridge, I didn't notice anybody standing inside, until my rock disappeared under the roof of the bridge, and I looked up. Someone about my age or a little older stood facing the other direction. Even in the shadows, I could tell it was a girl—the ponytail and puffy sleeve made that obvious.

I was determined not to get off on the wrong foot with this girl. "Hi," I said shyly. "I didn't see you there. Hope I didn't hit you with my rock."

She turned around. There was nothing female about the face that grinned at me, or the gruff voice. "Nay, you missed me by a furlong."

I was astonished. This was a boy all right, but he was wearing the weirdest clothes I'd ever seen. Besides the white shirt with billowy sleeves, he had on pants that ended at his knees, long white socks, and black shoes with big buckles. In his hand was a hat—a three-cornered hat.

Boy, Pennsylvania kids really go all out for Halloween, I thought. *And do they talk funny.* "Furlong?" I echoed, wondering if it meant *far* or *long* or what.

"Want to join me in a game of huzzlecap?" the boy said.

"Sure," I said, grateful for the invitation, even if I didn't know what it was for.

We fell into step and crossed the bridge. There we stopped. The kid put his hat down on the ground and took some coins from his pocket. "Huzzlecap's easy enough," he explained. "You need only pitch a farthing into the tricorne." His accent sounded as foreign as his words.

"Ah," I said, trying to sound as if I understood.

When the kid threw a coin at the three-cornered hat, I began to get an idea of what he meant, even though the coin didn't land anywhere near the target. "You...um...missed it by a furlong," I said.

"Aye, but it's a sight trickier than it looks. You try." He handed me one of the coins. I rubbed my finger over the raised letters: F-A-R-T-H-I-N-G. The rest of the letters were too worn to read, but now I remembered what a farthing was. I also recognized the boy's clipped accent. "Hey, are you British or something? My folks have been to England. They brought me back one of each kind of coin—a farthing, sort of like this one, and a tuppence, and even a ha'penny like in the 'Christmas Is A-Coming' song."

The boy looked at me with such an odd expression that I thought I'd put my foot in my mouth again.

I plunged on awkwardly. "You're not British, right? Sorry. I'm new here myself, and..." I figured I'd better change the subject. "Uh, I like your costume. Where did you get it?"

"My mother made it—from start to finish. It took her well nigh a fortnight just to weave the linsey-woolsey on her loom."

Again I was impressed by how much Pennsylvanians did for Halloween. Then I recalled that even in Minnesota, I knew some moms who were into weaving.

"What are you supposed to be?" I asked. My mother's words about Uncle George's long-haired phase popped into my head, and I made a wild guess. "A hippie?"

"Nay," said the boy with a smile and a shake of his head.

"Now, don't tell me—let me guess. Are you supposed to be George Washington? He wore a funny hat like that—but you know, your hair is all wrong. His was all curly and white."

The boy chuckled. "That was a wig, Lars. I feared you would be ignorant, but not as ignorant as that!"

My jaw must have dropped to my knees. "H-how did you know my name?" I managed to ask.

He picked up his hat and put the farthings in his pocket. "I heard your mother call you that," he said nonchalantly.

"But how did you hear..."

He ignored my question. "Come play ducks and drakes," he said. "Yonder's a prime spot for it— the run's wider there." He quickly walked toward the stream.

I followed, intrigued, and soon learned that *ducks and drakes* was his name for skipping rocks, something I was really good at, having grown up in the Land of Ten Thousand Lakes. My companion told me I was a "dab hand at ducks and drakes." I figured that was a compliment and returned it, because he was a good rock skipper, too. Unfortunately, he bounced away from my questions as expertly as he skipped stones.

After we were about skipped out, he turned to me and said, "'Tis good you've moved into Penncroft Farm." Suddenly he plucked the tricorne off his head and sailed it into the air. I dashed forward, caught it, and lobbed it back to him. We tossed the hat back and forth like a Frisbee until we reached the old split-rail fence bordering Penncroft Farm.

My new friend climbed up the zigzag rails and straddled the top. "It always seemed a waste of time to build fences around apple trees. They weren't about to run off. But the law said all farms had to be fenced. These stake-and-rider fences were the very devil to build, but they've weathered well," he remarked.

"Stake-and...?" I began, but just then I spotted my mom waiting at the end of the driveway by the Penncroft Farm sign. She was shading her eyes and looking anxiously down the road. When she saw me, she waved and started toward me.

"I've been waiting for you to get home, Lars," she said as she came closer. "How'd it go at school? Did you make any friends yet?"

"Well, yeah...*this* guy," I said, jabbing my thumb behind me toward the fence.

Mom looked where I'd pointed. She frowned. "What guy?"

"This guy right..." I whirled around. My newfound friend was nowhere to be seen. The stake-and-rider fence was riderless.

4

Raising the Shade

Saturday, I'd planned on sleeping in. But it was clear that my parents had different plans for me. At seven-thirty, my mother invaded my room.

"Time to get up, Lars. We need you to clean out the barn so we can stick the empty cartons in there."

"The whole barn? All by myself?" I squawked.

"Well, at least the ground floor," she said, relenting. "Be glad the barn's only half its original size. There used to be a whole other wing—the foundation's still there."

"What happened to it?" I murmured sleepily, playing for time.

"It caught on fire ages ago. Probably hit by lightning. The fire was put out, but only half the barn was saved."

Dad poked his head through the doorway. "Come on, Lars, hop to it. You've got to clear away the junk and rake out the barn. But do me a favor: Stay away from that wagon!"

I glanced guiltily at Dad and saw the meaningful look he exchanged with my mother.

"Guess I'll start on my study," he said, backing out again.

Mom sat down on my bed. "By the way, Lars, I want to talk with you about something." She cleared her throat. "I thought you'd outgrown imaginary friends."

"But Mom, there really *was* a kid on the fence!" I protested. "I met him on the road."

"Then he disappeared into thin air, like the guy at the window and the mysterious superhero on the wagon," she said with a skeptical smile. "Now look, honey, I know you've been through a lot and really miss your old friends, but you'll make new friends sooner than you think. So please give up this imaginary stuff and don't pester Aunt Cass with such nonsense, okay?"

I grunted. Luckily, she took that for a sign of agreement. As she got up to leave, her glance fell on the space next to old George's portrait. "Think I'll fill that empty spot with a map of Pennsylvania," she said. "But what a shame to break up the Peale paintings. From what Aunt Cass says, George's wife was quite a fascinating woman. You wouldn't believe what she did during the Revolution!"

I yawned and pulled the covers over my head. Mom pulled them right off again. "I'm not leaving this room until you're vertical!" she said sternly, planting her hands on her hips.

"I'm vertical, I'm vertical!" I retorted, climbing reluctantly out of bed.

After Mom left, I pulled on my jeans and rummaged through cartons looking for my Minnesota Twins sweatshirt. It was easy for Mom to say I'd have new friends soon—she didn't know what a disaster my first day had been. I'd only given her the usual string of *fines* when she'd asked how things had gone.

At least I had a whole weekend before I had to face those kids again. Even raking out the barn was better than that.

Aunt Cass was in the kitchen when I got there. She placed a bowl of oatmeal and a small blue pitcher of thick cream on the table and asked me if I'd slept well.

"Yup. My bed wasn't too short, wasn't too long," I joked. "In fact, it was ju-u-u-st right!"

"Funny how that happens sometimes," she replied, her face perfectly straight. She sat down next to me.

I shook my spoon at her. "Not all *that* funny!" I said. For the next few minutes I wolfed down oatmeal, Aunt Cass watching with a look of satisfaction. I decided to ignore Mom's instructions about pestering my great-aunt.

"You know, my bed's not the only funny thing around here," I began tentatively. "There was that guy I saw in the window, and then yesterday I met someone who did an incredible disappearing act. One second he was there; the next, he wasn't!"

Aunt Cass gazed at me. "What'd he look like?" she asked in a low voice.

"It's a little hard to say. He was all dressed up for Halloween in a George Washington costume. And there was something else funny about him: He knew my name. He said he heard Mom call me that, so he must live really close by. Do you know who he could be?"

She nodded slowly. "Ye-e-s, perhaps I do, but I wouldn't exactly say he *lives* around here."

"Oh," I said, disappointed. "I was hoping he might be somebody to hang out with."

"What about Pat Hargreaves?" she said, her

mouth quirking up at the corners. "Didn't you meet her at school yesterday? Come on, George—don't tell me you don't like Pat just because she's a girl!"

"She's all right, Aunt Cass, but..."

"Good, because she'll be here later this morning. Her folks are coming over to do me a favor, and I expect you to be hospitable."

"Yeah, okay," I said. I cleared my dishes and headed outside to the barn.

The wooden sides of the barn—or what was left of it—were weathered to a gray that matched the foundation stones. There was a full top story, but because the barn was set into the hill, the ground floor was only about the size of our Minneapolis garage, much to my relief.

A wide door ran across the lower level. I gave it a shove, and the door creaked open on ancient iron hinges. I entered the dark inside, groping for a light switch as I went. I couldn't find one.

"Swell. How can I clean this place if I can't see what I'm doing?" I asked, wasting good sarcasm on an empty barn. Moving gingerly along the wall, I touched a large, round, metallic object that felt nothing like a light switch. It clattered to the floor. I slid my foot around until I found it, then carried it across to the door for a closer look. It was a flat metal sieve, covered with cobwebs, red with rust, and bigger than any sieve I'd ever seen.

Perplexed, I murmured, "I'd hate to have to eat any macaroni that was strained in this... this... *whatever* it is!"

"'Tis a riddle," said a voice in my ear.

I whirled around. It was the kid I'd met at the bridge.

"Why, you're still dressed up as Washington!" I exclaimed.

The boy's bright blue eyes crinkled with amusement. "'Tis my only costume. My mother had little time to make me fancy duds."

"I know what you mean. My mom's never been much for sewing, either," I said, relieved to have some common ground with this guy. "She'd rather spend her spare time reading."

"Aye, Sandra always did have her nose in a book. Me, I never cottoned much to anything but ciphering—doing sums and such—when I was your age. I did learn reading properly enough later on," he said proudly.

He doesn't look all that much older than me, I thought indignantly. Then what he'd said about ciphering sank in and I perked up. Maybe I'd found somebody who liked secret codes as much as I did, though I'd never heard of using addition to break one. Eagerly, I turned to him and asked if he went to my school.

"Nay, nor any other. My mother learned me with a hornbook."

"You lucky dog! Wish *I* didn't have to, especially here in *Pennsylvania*." I started to make a face, but remembered this kid was as Pennsylvanian as the ones at school. "Ah, you left so . . . so suddenly yesterday that I didn't get a chance to ask what your name is," I said, feeling awkward.

"My name's Geordie," he said, looking amused.

"How do you do, Gordie."

"No, Lars, not *Gordie*—my name's *Geordie*."

"Geordie. How do you do?" I reached out to shake hands.

But instead of shaking hands, Geordie went all stiff and bent over in a bow like the ones my piano teacher made us do in recitals. I went still, too—from amazement. Then, feeling self-conscious, I bowed back. As I bent over, I noticed I was still holding the rusty old sieve in my left hand. "Now, about this . . . riddle, Geordie, I guess I just don't get what you mean."

Geordie took the sieve and turned it over

thoughtfully. I noticed that his fingernails were bitten to the quick.

"'Tis a riddle—leastwise, that's what we always called it," he explained. "It's for cleaning all the dirt and dust out of wheat. Aye, I spent many a winter evening shaking this riddle. Actually, I much preferred my outdoor tasks, like making perry in the fall when the picking was done."

"Making what?"

"The perry—cider made from pears instead of apples. A hard cider, fermented into alcohol," Geordie said. "And there were plenty of other chores to do—picking apples and pruning trees and all the other farm and orchard tasks. Then, after my brother, Will, left home, I also had to deliver the perry and cider and fruit to the inns and take it into Philadelphia on market days. 'Twas difficult, but Father insisted I was grown enough to shoulder my brother's work as well as my own."

I nodded emphatically. "I know what you mean. I got the same routine after Peter moved out. 'You're the chief helper, now, Lars.' Besides, lucky Peter gets to stay in Minnesota." The realization hit me that if I'd stayed in Minnesota, I wouldn't have met Geordie. Maybe Peter wasn't so lucky after all.

"Where did your brother go, Geordie? Off to college, like Peter?" I asked.

"Nay, college was too dear for the likes of us," he replied.

I wondered briefly if *dear* was some Pennsylvania way of saying *neat,* like we used to say *sweet* back in Minnesota. But that didn't make any sense, either. "What do you mean by *dear,* Geordie?"

"'Twas too costly, too expensive," he said softly.

"Didn't your brother apply for a scholarship?"

"Nay, Will went off to be a soldier, in '77. My father nearly had apoplexy when he heard tell of it—he was that furious. But Will was set on fighting in the war, and there was no stopping him—not our Will. We always used to say, 'Where there's a Will, there's a way.'"

"B-but Uncle George was killed at the *end* of Vietnam, and that was *way* before 1977," I said, bewildered.

"'Twas the War of Independency, Lars," Geordie said quietly. "And the year Will went away was 1777," he added, giving me an almost sympathetic look.

My knees buckled and I sank down onto the dirt floor. "You don't . . . you can't mean the American Revolution?" My voice rose into a squeak.

"Aye—against the English king, George III. Father was a loyalist and railed against what he called 'ragtag traitors' who demanded Independency. He said the king only wanted us to pay our fair share for the British troops he'd sent to defend us from the Indians and the French. As a lad, Father himself had taken up his musket to fight the French for the king. But Will said taxing us without our say was tyranny."

I sat on the floor, gasping like a beached whale.

Geordie quickly went on. "You see, up until then, Americans had always raised their own money. That way, even though the royal governors were officially in charge, they couldn't carry out anything the Americans didn't want to pay for. But if Parliament could tax Americans directly, the royal governors would control the purse strings and could do whatever they liked. That's what Will called tyranny." Geordie sighed. "How Father hated to hear him say that. From way up at the house, Mother and I could hear them arguing in the orchard. We joked that it would sour the fruit, but no jokes could help heal the wounds in our family. That's why Will finally ran away to join George Washington."

"To join George Washington," I echoed, dazed.

"Aye. As for my mother, it was like to tear her apart, her being raised a Friend and all. Though she was disowned by the meeting for marrying Father, she was still a Quaker at heart. Quakers believe all killing wrong, even in war. They're pacifists."

"I knew that," I chimed in, glad that something he said sounded familiar.

"Anyway, in Mother's eyes, it was bad enough for Will to take up arms against another human being. For him to fly in the face of Pa's loyalty to England as well nearly split our family like a piece of kindling wood."

A wild thought flitted through my head: Maybe this was a trick that someone at school, like the Owens kid, had put this boy up to to make a fool of me. But there was something about Geordie that made what he said almost believable.

Suddenly the implications of his words struck me, if not dumb, at least into a whisper. "B-but if you were alive during the Revolution, you must be the oldest person in the world!"

It was Geordie's turn to look taken aback. He actually blushed a little as he tried to explain. "Well, that's not exactly accurate, Lars. I'm actually a phantasm."

"A phantasm?" I repeated, mystified. "What's that?"

"Some would say an apparition," Geordie said. "Do you know what that is?"

I shook my head.

Geordie sighed. "I had this same problem with your uncle George when he was your age. He insisted on calling me a ghost, which I thought was dreadful. The word *ghost* makes people think of rattling chains and cobwebs and such." He indicated the cobwebs on the riddle with a shudder. "If it's all the same to you, I'd rather be called a shade. That means the same thing as ghost but sounds a mite more amiable, don't you think?" he asked rather wistfully.

I didn't have an opinion on the subject, but since it seemed to matter to him, I nodded. "Now, let me get this straight," I said, determined to be calm. "You're a ghost—pardon me, I mean a shade—and you haunt our house. Is that right?"

Geordie picked at the cobwebs on the riddle for a moment before he looked up. "I haunt your *barn*, actually, with the odd trip into the house now and again, like the night you arrived."

That roused me from my stupor. "Was that *you*

up there?" Seeing Geordie's nod, I jumped to my feet. "So it *was* a shade I saw in the window—but not the kind Mom thought it was!" I laughed. "And what Uncle George told Mom wasn't a tall tale. Penncroft Farm *is* haunted, just like Uncle George said. Even the *wagon*'s haunted!"

Geordie bashfully dug the toe of his buckled shoe into the straw-littered dirt of the floor. "I'd be gratified, Lars, if you wouldn't say *haunt*. I prefer to think of it as hanging out."

I looked at him in surprise. "Really? Hanging out?"

"Aye, and the barn always was my favorite place to hang out, ever since the raising," he said enthusiastically.

"The raising?" Curious as I was how Geordie had risen from the dead or whatever and had come to haunt Penncroft Farm, I didn't really want to hear the gory details. I told him firmly that he didn't have to tell me about the raising if it was too painful.

"I mean the *barn* raising, you sapskull!" Geordie said with a lopsided grin. "Nothing the least bit painful about it. People came from miles around to help raise the ridgepole and put up the walls. 'Twas a great deal of fun!"

"Doesn't sound like much fun—all that work," I put in.

"It wasn't just work. We had all manner of diversions, and feasted on apple pie and mulled cider and good roast beef. Of course, the best part was the labyrinth the older lads made out of hay over yonder in the south meadow. I was so young, I was barely out of leading strings, but I reached the end of the maze before anyone else. I was right proud." Geordie stopped, a faraway look in his eyes. "The only part of the raising I didn't like was the husking bee, a kind of a party," he said. "We all sat about pulling the husks from the ears of corn. It was my terrible misfortune to husk an entirely red ear." He gave me a significant look.

I gave him back a blank one. "A red ear? I don't get it."

"Whoever husked a red ear got kissed by *all* the girls! When I saw I'd husked one, Will saw it, too; he whistled to call attention to the fact." He grinned. "Will had the loudest, most piercing whistle you can imagine. Mother said he could out-whistle the wind and forbade him doing so indoors. But Mother wasn't husking corn that day, so Will whistled until everybody screamed and covered their ears. That gave me a chance to ease out the toad I happened to have in my pocket. When I held it up by my face, all those lasses thought the better of kissing me, I assure you. Will's whistle and their squealing nearly raised the new barn roof off the ridgepole!" he said, tossing the riddle to me.

I decided that a raising must have been more fun than I'd thought. "Geordie," I asked lobbing him the riddle with a laugh, "did you have another raising to rebuild the barn after part of it burned?"

Geordie's face turned sober. "No, times weren't right for a party, and . . . well, we just fixed it as best we could. Made it smaller—like it is now."

"No mulled cider or apple pie? No husking bee?" I asked.

Geordie crowed, "And no red ears or kissing girls!"

Our laughter threatened to raise the roof yet again, but we abruptly stopped when we heard Dad's voice.

"Lars! What are you up to in there? Sounds like a pack of hyenas!" he said, coming through the barn door.

Some instinct sent me leaping across to stand in front of Geordie. My father frowned and asked, "What's that?"

For a second, I thought he was asking about

Geordie, and I was awash in panic, but his eyes were on the rusty sieve in my hands. "It's a riddle to me, Dad," I said solemnly.

"What's a riddle to *me* is what you've been doing out here all this time. You haven't even turned the light on yet!"

"Couldn't find the switch," I mumbled.

"That's because there isn't one. You just pull this cord hanging down from the lightbulb, here in the middle."

The barn was flooded with light. Holding my breath, I looked carefully around. Geordie was nowhere to be seen. Whistling with relief, I walked over and put the riddle back on a large wooden peg jutting from the wall. I figured it must have been hanging there when I dislodged it in the dark.

Dad was looking at me kind of funny. "Your moods certainly shift gears in a hurry lately, Lars. Your mother said you were depressed, and here you are grinning away like a Cheshire cat." He shrugged. "Look, I have to run some errands. I want you finished here by the time I get back. Now rake up this old straw and put it in garbage bags to take to the dump. Better toss in that sieve, too."

I snatched the riddle off its peg and held it to my chest protectively. "Can't I keep it?"

"I guess so, but check with Aunt Cass before you take it in the house. No telling what it's been used for."

"No telling," I echoed with a grin as I watched him get in the car with Mom and drive away. After they were out of sight, I picked up the rake and pitched in. Somehow cleaning the barn didn't seem so boring after all.

5

Bamboozling Aunt Cass

After I finished in the barn, I picked up the old sieve and headed for the house, ready to pop with excitement about my experience with Geordie. Remembering how I'd boggled at the riderless fence, I punned, "That's one riddle solved!"

Inside, I found Aunt Cass scribbling on a pad of yellow legal paper, which she quickly turned over when she saw me.

I plopped the riddle down on the table next to her. "Do you like riddles as much as you like puns?" I asked.

Aunt Cass picked up the sieve, which left a rusty outline on the tablecloth. Instead of chewing me out for making a mess, she only said, "Yes, I..." But whatever she'd intended to say was broken off by the sound of a car pulling up. "That's the Hargreaveses' van!" she exclaimed, taking my arm and half dragging me out to meet the visitors. My reluctance must have been obvious to Pat Hargreaves, who, after hugging my great-aunt, glanced at me and turned red.

"Hello, Ellen," Aunt Cass said. "Sorry to take you away from your Saturday chores, Will, but this is important." She made the introductions, then with a significant look at me, added, "Of course, George and Pat have already met. Why don't you two youngsters take a walk? We have some business to attend to."

Not very enthusiastically, I took off toward the barn. Pat fell into step beside me. Without speaking, we marched past the wagon in the lean-to and stopped by the pond.

"How about some ducks and drakes?" I asked.

Her brown eyes opened wide. "What?"

"Ducks and drakes. Somebody told me that's what you call skipping rocks around here."

She shrugged. "As Aunt Cass would say, somebody's been bamboozling you, Lars. Was it Eddie? He loves teasing new kids—probably because he's so out of it himself."

"Nope, not Eddie," I replied calmly, though inside I felt like shouting in celebration. If Pat Hargreaves had never heard of ducks and drakes, she had probably never met Geordie. Grinning, I picked up a stone and tried to skip it on the water. It skittered about one inch and sank. I tried again. This time the rock didn't even skitter—it just sank.

Pat squatted down by the edge of the pond, picked up several stones, examined them, and tossed them back down. Finally finding one that suited her, she turned it over a couple of times to fit into her hand properly, then flung it at the pond. It skipped a good six or seven times.

Maybe Pat didn't know that skipping rocks was called ducks and drakes, but she was what Geordie would call a "dab hand" at it. "That wasn't too shabby—for a girl," I said.

Pat tossed her head. "It wasn't too shabby, *period!*"

I picked up another rock, and, determined not to be outdone by a girl, hurled it with everything I had. It skipped about ten times—my best throw ever. "How about *that*?" I asked proudly.

"How about *what*? I was looking for another rock and wasn't watching," she said airily, playing with the ring on her chain.

I shook my head in disgust. "You girls always have some excuse when you're beaten," I declared.

She put her hands on her hips and glared at me. "Look, Lars, there's no reason for you to have a chip on your shoulder."

"That's easy for *you* to say. *You* don't have to move. *You* don't have to make new friends."

"I certainly don't!" She whirled and ran toward the house.

I felt like kicking myself. Instead, I tore off after her, but by the time I came around the barn, she was already in the van. Her parents were outside talking to Aunt Cass.

"Oh, there you are, George. Just in time to say good-bye." She turned back to speak to the Hargreaveses. "Thanks again for coming over. I needed signatures of someone outside the family; although, loosely speaking, you're in the family."

"We tenth cousins are always happy to help, Cass. But shouldn't you get a lawyer to read it?" asked Mr. Hargreaves.

"No. Ebenezer Bank told me it was perfectly legal if it's signed by two witnesses, and even they don't have to read it. I have an idea. Why don't you come to our party tonight? I'm sure Sandra and Erik would like to see you, and Lars would certainly have a better time with Patience than with grown-ups."

I glanced at Pat to see if she understood what Aunt Cass was talking about. My mom was always telling me to be more patient, but how was that better than being with grown-ups?

Pat looked as confused as I was, if not more so.

"I'm sorry, Cass," said Mrs. Hargreaves, "but we have a meeting to go to, and Pat has other plans. Otherwise we would've loved to come. Wouldn't we, honey?"

Pat gave a minimal nod. Her parents quickly got in the van, and they drove off.

After they were out of sight, Aunt Cass looked at me. "Well, George," she said, "what do you want to dress up as tonight?"

"I'm too old to wear a costume for Halloween," I answered.

"Nonsense. If *I'm* still young enough to do it, so are you!"

She put her hand on my arm and gave it a little squeeze. "Don't worry, George, you won't look any sillier than the rest of us."

"I don't wear costumes. Period," I said dully.

She let my elbow drop. "Okay. I give up. I'm sure we'll still have a good time. We'll pull out all the stops!"

She wasn't kidding. We did actually pull out all

the stops—on her pump organ, that is. We pulled all the organ's knobs out until it was so loud the wavy old glass windowpanes rattled. As I pumped and she played, I told Aunt Cass about the Nautilus exercise machine/submarine pun I'd thought of the first time we'd met—only a few days before, but it seemed like a lifetime. She liked my joke, and proved it by playing the Captain Nemo piece. Duddle-la... deedle deedle deet deeeeee.

My mother, rigged out as Mae West, came and tapped me on the shoulder. "Do you have to play that organ so loud? It's deafening!"

"Don't be a party pooper, Sandra," Aunt Cass said, her fingers flying over the keyboard. "I'm sure Mae West never was."

Mom pointed at Cass's old black dress. "Judge Bank will be here any minute, and you're not even in costume yet!"

"Ah, but I am! I only need my makeup and hat to be ready," Aunt Cass said. She peered at me. "I told Ebenezer not to come without a costume. I don't think much of a man who's too proud to put on silly clothes once in a while; there's nothing like a little foolishness to take one's pride down a peg or two."

"What?" I asked, feeling uncomfortable.

"That's just an expression, honey," Mom explained. "To take someone down a peg means to humble him a little."

Dad came into the room, dressed as Robin Hood in Sherwood Forest—green long johns that were silly enough to meet with Aunt Cass's full approval. Raising his eyebrows under his feathered hat, he exclaimed, "Funny how Lars has always hated wearing costumes!"

Mom frowned in my general direction. "Well, he'll just miss out on some of the fun," she said, then shooed Aunt Cass down the hall to finish dressing.

While they were gone, Dad cleared his throat the way he always does when he starts one of his "man-to-man" speeches. "I would think you could make an effort, Lars. After all, Aunt Cass won't have too many more Halloweens to celebrate. If your mother and I can dress up to please her, I should think you could . . ."

I was saved by the knocker. At the door was an elderly, dignified man dressed formally in a tuxedo, a top hat, and a pig's snout. It was Aunt Cass's old friend Judge Ebenezer Bank.

My mother came out to greet him and babbled on about how long it had been and all that stuff.

Finally, she introduced us. I looked at my blonde-wigged mother, my long-johned father, and our pig-faced guest and felt a little embarrassed for them. Suddenly, Aunt Cass made a grand entrance through the arched doorway. Apple-green makeup covered her face, a witch's hat sat on her white hair, and in her hand was a large picnic basket. She struck a menacing pose. "And your little dog, too," she cackled.

I looked at her smiling green face, crinkled with age and laugh lines, and wondered how I'd ever thought she looked like Dorothy's witch. Toto would have eaten right out of her hand.

That Halloween party was a strange mixture of fun and solemnity, just like Aunt Cass herself. Although we joked a lot as we popped corn in the old wire popper and roasted apples over the coals in the huge old fireplace, the grown-ups would sometimes forget their weird appearances and plunge into serious topics.

Finally, as she stirred hot spiced cider in the big copper kettle in a pretty witchy way, Aunt Cass said, "You know, people keep moaning gloom and doom about how horrible everything is now and mooning on about the good old days." She sniffed. "The good old days were just as mixed a bag as any other days, old or new. And yet we muddled through." She pointed a knobby finger at me. "That's the value of history, L. George. Don't you forget it. People have always managed to muddle through, and I believe they always will. I guess it's human nature to forget the bad times, gloss 'em over, shine 'em up, and put 'em all neat and clean in the history books." She absentmindedly scratched her head, knocking her witch's hat askew.

Judge Bank took the last bite of his pumpkin pie and leaned back in his fireside chair. "By the way, Cass, I saw the Hargreaveses this afternoon and they said you'd made a new will. I wish you'd let me take a look to make sure it's done properly."

My parents sat up a little straighter in the settles.

"Oh, don't fuss about it, Eb. It's almost like my old one. I just had to change a thing or two."

"But you shouldn't keep it around here. It should be in a safety deposit box," Dad said.

Judge Bank humphed. "Just you try to get her to keep anything in a safety deposit box! I've been trying for years, but no—Cass has some hidey-hole that beats the bank!"

"I've always said that yours was the only bank I trusted, Eb," Cass said, giving the judge's hand an affectionate pat.

"It's all very well to joke, Cass, but I think you should at least tell someone where it is."

"That won't be necessary. Wild Indians couldn't drag it out of me. No, not even extremely civil Indians could make me tell." Aunt Cass's eyes turned to meet mine. "But someone with the right *spirit* could find it."

"It won't be wild Indians who have to look for it if something should happen to you."

Aunt Cass hesitated. "Oh, all right, Eb. I'll put it wherever you like on Monday. But I don't plan to die for a good long while. After all, I just got to know George here. I'm looking forward to watching him grow up—at least a little. Besides, I'm so relieved that the three of you are here," she went on. "It'll help me out of a muddle. There's this fellow who kept shining up to me, saying as how he'd turn Penncroft into a museum of the First American Civil War. Well, all he really wanted was to glorify his own set of ancestors—who were nothing to crow about. I tried to tell him that wasn't what I had in mind, but he wouldn't listen." As Aunt Cass spoke, she looked more and more agitated. Once again she put her hand to her heart, and her face looked pale in the spots that weren't green.

Dad volunteered me to do the dishes, and I

went without my usual squawk. As I washed and dried the plates, I thought about what Dad had said about Aunt Cass not having many more Halloweens to look forward to. When I'd finished, I went upstairs to my room. I looked hurriedly through the cartons next to the wall but found nothing I could use for a costume. I threw myself facedown on the bed and tried to think.

At last an idea hit me. I ran to the linen closet, took out an old sheet and cut eyeholes in it with my pocketknife. Then I foraged around in Mom's room and found some blue eye stuff to smear around my eyes, where it would show through the eyeholes. Finally, draping the sheet over myself, I slunk downstairs.

Aunt Cass was playing the organ again and no one heard me coming, especially since Judge Bank was singing along, off-key. Duddle-la... deedle deedle deet deeeeee. It was perfect mood music for what I planned to do. I slipped out the back door and hustled around to the front; the cold October wind whipped the sheet wildly about my ankles. I lifted the knocker and let it fall three times. The music stopped. I held my breath, waiting for the door to open. It didn't.

"Guess they didn't hear the knocker after all," I

muttered. My teeth started to chatter in the cold night air. Then I decided that an unannounced entrance might be more effective, anyway. I opened the door with the latchstring and swooped inside, swirling around the living room oohing and booing like crazy. I could hardly wait to see Aunt Cass's face when she realized who this guest ghost was.

Nobody reacted. Nobody at all. I was so blinded by the sheet that it wasn't until I heard my mother sobbing and whispering Cass's name over and over that I knew something was wrong. I struggled out of the sheet.

Aunt Cass was lying on the floor in front of the organ. My dad was doing CPR on her while Mom hovered frantically nearby. Judge Bank spoke tersely into the telephone, giving directions for an ambulance.

Mom lifted tear-filled eyes to me. "Lars, give me that sheet to cover her. She may go into shock."

I stood by in a kind of shock myself as Mom and Dad took turns trying to revive Aunt Cass.

Finally her eyelids fluttered open. "George," she said weakly. "George."

I leaned over her. "Aunt Cass. I dressed up for you. See?" I motioned down, then remembered I wasn't wearing the sheet anymore.

She managed a weak smile and repeated my name, or at least my middle name. Her eyes closed again as the ambulance arrived.

We were so worried about Aunt Cass that none of us thought how odd we looked trooping into the emergency room at the hospital in our costumes.

Mom went in to be with Aunt Cass while the doctors examined her, leaving the three of us standing in the waiting room. My teeth were chattering again, this time from emotion. In fact, I was shaking all over.

Judge Bank patted my shoulder. "Your great-aunt has had a bad heart for years, Lars. She didn't want anybody to know about it—she hates being fussed over. The doctor told her that any agitation could bring on a heart attack, but Cass said if she had to sit in a rocker and try not to feel anything—no anger, no joy—well, that wouldn't feel much like being alive."

Dad ruffled my hair. "She's had a long, happy life, Lars."

Mom came out of the swinging door, her painted Mae West face looking weird under the fluorescent lights. Without a word, she pulled off her wig and came over to hug Dad and me. Then she said, shakily, "She seems to be doing better than they would expect for a woman her age. She's resting now."

"Can I see her?" I asked eagerly.

"Afraid not, honey. But she told me to give you a message."

A lump rose in my throat.

"It didn't make a lot of sense. She said something about a riddle and taking you down a peg. I guess she meant how you dressed up just to make her happy, when she knew how much you didn't want to." Mom burst into tears.

Just then a nurse came running out to get us. Aunt Cass had suffered another heart attack and could not be revived.

It was very late when I dragged up the stairs to my room. Hardly aware of what I was doing, I started to slide into bed. Halfway down, my feet struck the carefully shorted sheet and stuck fast.

"Bamboozled again," I said in a choked voice, and cried myself to sleep under the canopy.

6

The Riddle Song

When the bus door swung open, I climbed up the steps, feeling as if I were stuck in a nightmare.

The driver whistled cheerfully. "Happy Monday morning," he said. "Did you have a good Halloween?"

I couldn't talk about what had happened on Halloween so I nodded silently and made my way to the back of the bus.

Over my protests, my parents had packed me off to school. They would be gone all morning making arrangements for Aunt Cass's memorial service. They said school would keep me occupied.

Actually, I thought, *occupied* wasn't a bad way to describe the situation—like an enemy army occupies the land of the loser. At least the events of the weekend made my school problems seem less important. Compared with the shock of losing Aunt Cass, facing Eddie Owens was nothing.

The bus stopped and Pat Hargreaves got on. I noticed that her eyes were swollen, then I deliberately turned my head away and watched the bare-limbed trees moving by. I felt the seat sink a little and turned to find Pat sitting beside me. The last thing I needed was a sympathetic face. I knew it would probably upset me, which would hardly repair my bad start at school.

"I heard what happened on Halloween," she said softly.

"I'd rather not talk about it, Pat. Look, do you have to sit here?" I asked. My voice, hoarse with emotion, made my words sound gruffer than I intended.

"You're not the only one who misses her," said Pat, getting to her feet. She put her hand to her eyes and stumbled across the aisle to sit down on the other side.

Gradually the bus filled up. My expression seemed to keep the other kids at a distance; no one tried to share my seat, which suited me fine. As we reached the town, however, a shrill voice broke through my thoughts.

"Well, if it isn't the Norweirdgian!"

There could be no doubt who the speaker was: Edward Owens the Tenth, as obnoxious in regular clothes as in his cowboy rig.

I ignored him. Unfortunately, that didn't discourage him; it egged him on.

"Bet nobody came trick-or-treating to *your* house. Everyone says it's haunted because of that old witch Cass Hargreaves."

Quick as a flash, Pat Hargreaves flew across the aisle and slapped Eddie Owens.

"Wh-what did you do that for?" Eddie stammered.

"Because you deserved it!" Pat cried. She returned to her seat as quickly as she had left it, her face as red as an apple.

Eddie looked as if he didn't know what had hit him, even if he did know *who*. He was stunned into silence. That was fine with me. In a way, it was the most pleasant time I had spent in his company. It didn't last very long.

"Bet I got more stuff trick-or-treating than you did." He patted his backpack smugly.

I shrugged. "Didn't go out. We had a family party at home."

"Sounds bo-o-ring!" Eddie said in a nerdy sing-song.

More than anything, I wanted to sock him. Then I remembered Aunt Cass and felt all mixed-up inside. Even though I ached about her death, I could still feel furious. It was like being two different people at once. I gritted my teeth and didn't move.

When he didn't get any reaction from me, Eddie got bored. "I'm going up to see how the other guys did trick-or-treating. The ones whose mothers didn't keep 'em at home for a boring Norweirdgian family party!"

"That's *Norwegian*," I hissed, clenching my fists.

Eddie swaggered up the aisle. I saw him try to squeeze in with two boys about halfway to the front, but they shoved him away. He tried to do the same with some kids across the aisle, but they didn't want him sharing their seat, either. Eddie sneaked a look back at me. I felt smug and let him see it. He slunk into the only empty spot—next to a girl.

All my smugness fell away as the school came into view. With growing nervousness, I joined the current of kids that flowed off the bus, up the stairs, and down the hall, splitting off at each classroom door.

Surrounded by other students noisily comparing notes on their trick-or-treating hauls, I silently hung up my coat and took my seat. My brain was racing, anticipating the day ahead. At least I would be leaving early; the memorial service was right after school and I had a note explaining that Mom would pick me up at two. Unfortunately, there was still plenty of time to get into trouble with my "new friends" at school.

Then I remembered Geordie, and the thought that I *did* have a friend—and a special one at that—gave me a spurt of self-confidence. *After all,* I said to myself, glancing around at the others, *who else in this whole school has his own personal—now what was it Geordie wanted to be called?* Shade, *that was it!—who else here has his own personal shade to talk to?*

For an instant, I considered telling the other kids about Geordie, but I hated to resort to the kind of boasting that made Eddie Owens so obnoxious. Besides, they would only think I was making it up.

Mrs. Hettrick stood up. "All right, class. We have a little business concerning Colonial Day. So far, we have committees handling food and crafts projects, and you're working in gym on the Virginia reel..." She paused for a moment to allow for the boys' groans. "And I presume each of you is working on a costume." She gave me a quick, inquiring glance. "Now don't forget to pick an authentic colonial name to use for the day, like *Prudence* or *Patience*."

I happened to catch Pat Hargreaves's eye. At the teacher's words, she flushed and looked away. *She must still be upset over the way I acted on the bus,* I thought as I focused again on the teacher.

"Anyway," Mrs. Hettrick went on, "the planners think we should have one more major activity for Colonial Day. They've come up with an excellent idea: a husking bee! You know, in colonial days, young people loved going to husking bees!"

I thought of Geordie's ordeal and smirked. "Not *all* young people," I muttered.

Mrs. Hettrick asked if anyone knew what a husking bee was, but not a hand was raised—except mine. The teacher looked at me in surprise. "Lars? Do *you* know?"

I nodded, embarrassed.

With an encouraging smile, Mrs. Hettrick asked me to tell the rest of the class what a husking bee was.

I cleared my throat and began to talk, very qui-

etly. "A husking bee was wh
to husk corn. It was a kind of
could have fun while they got s
done."

"And?" prompted Mrs. Hettrick. "V
so much fun? Sitting around pulling husk
sounds dreary."

I swallowed and glanced nervously at
faces turned toward me. "And . . . and . . . and if yo
husked a red ear of corn, there were penalties to be
paid."

"Like trick or treat? I did some great tricks on
Halloween!" put in the seldom speechless Eddie.

For once I was more than happy to have him
horn in, but Mrs. Hettrick frowned away the
interruption.

"And what was the penalty to be paid?" she
asked.

"K-k-kisses," I stammered, feeling my ears turn
as red as any corn.

The class erupted.

"Kisses! No way! *I'm* not kissing anybody!"
hooted the other boys, while the girls giggled and
nudged each other.

Mrs. Hettrick waved her hands in the air for silence. "Okay, okay, you've convinced me! We'll skip

to think of another
ͻ"

in the air. "How
used to make
in at harvest
an *amazing*
out of my
hich made
surrounded

en people got together
party—so that they
ome boring work
hat made it
s off corn
the

...ick started handing out some pa-
. This is a quiz about the battle at Brandywine
Creek, to make sure you know the important facts
about it before our field trip there. Lars, you don't
have to take this. Use it as a study sheet."

Eddie Owens's hand waved in the air. "Do I get
any extra points for writing about my ancestor at
Brandywine?" he asked.

Another groan rose from the rest of the class. It
was different from the one after my pun. "Here he
goes again," someone said disgustedly. That didn't
faze Eddie.

"Well, you know, the Americans were trying to
stop the British from capturing Philadelphia, and
Dad says our ancestor rode like Paul Revere to

warn Washington that the British were sneaking across the upper fords and . . ."

"Eddie, this is testing time, not show-and-tell," said Mrs. Hettrick sternly. "You're giving away important answers."

There was a rustling noise as everyone took a sudden interest in Eddie, who peered around suspiciously, then muttered, "Yeah, well, I'll still get the highest grade. My dad has told me all about the Revolution."

Mrs. Hettrick sighed. "I'm sure he has, Eddie," she said wearily, "but please just write down your answers and show me what you *do* know."

Then I remembered my mother's note, and a fresh wave of sadness broke over me. Without a word, I handed the envelope to Mrs. Hettrick, and she scanned the page.

"Oh, Lars!" she exclaimed, turning to me. "I'm so sorry to hear about your great-aunt—a wonderful lady! How sad that you've only just moved in with her and now she's died."

"Died!" Eddie yelped behind me. "Wait till I tell my dad!"

The look on Mrs. Hettrick's face made me hope, for a brief moment, that she might give

Eddie the same treatment as Pat had. It was a little disappointing when she collected herself and merely told him to get to work.

I turned to the chapter on Brandywine and tried to read it, but the words blurred on the page. It might as well have been ciphering for all the sense I could make of it—or of anything else that long, long day.

When Mom picked me up that afternoon, I asked nervously what the funeral would be like.

"It's a memorial service, not a funeral," she said, giving my hand a reassuring pat. "A time for friends to get together and remember Aunt Cass."

Recalling my first long talk with my great-aunt, I murmured, "Friends, Quakers, or friends, *amigos*?"

"Both," Mom answered. We rode along in silence for a few miles. Then she cleared her throat. "Look, honey, try not to grieve for Aunt Cass too much. She wouldn't have wanted you to. Just be glad you had the chance to get to know her and to bring her joy. And you did. Great joy."

I interlocked my fingers and squeezed my hands together so as not to cry. Soon we pulled into a parking lot and stopped in front of a simple stone house with a slate roof.

"This doesn't look like a church," I said. "It

doesn't have stained-glass windows or a steeple or anything."

"It isn't a church, silly. It's a meetinghouse. Come on."

I hung back a little, worrying about what was going to happen. I shouldn't have been. Inside were several rows of chairs in a large circle. A few people sat quietly with heads bowed. I recognized only one—Judge Bank's.

My mother guided me to a chair in the front row and sat down beside me. Dad came up and asked in a whisper if I was all right. He saw my nod and sat down on the other side of Mom.

People started to filter in, greeting one another in hushed voices. Just before the time set for the service to begin, the Hargreaveses came in. My mother motioned them to join us and Pat sank into the chair next to me.

We all sat in silence. My heart was thudding so loudly it seemed as if everyone would hear it in the quiet room. I wondered when the minister would come in and start the service.

Suddenly Mr. Hargreaves stood up. "Let us be thankful for having Cass live among us for so long. She was a good friend," he said, his deep voice ringing out in the meeting room.

"Is Mr. Hargreaves the minister?" I asked Mom softly.

"There isn't any minister. Everybody says what he feels. About Cass."

"Oh." I thought about this for a moment, then whispered again, nervously, "Am *I* supposed to say something, too?"

"Only if you want to."

Other people stood up and talked about Aunt Cass. But it seemed to me that the person they were talking about was very different from the mischievous old lady I had known for so short a time.

Then Judge Bank rose to tell about his long friendship with Cass Hargreaves. I could hardly believe that this tall, solemn man was the same one who had worn a pig's snout to please Aunt Cass. It was as if he were a different person altogether.

A different person altogether, I thought. That was it. Each person here saw a slightly different side of Aunt Cass. Now we were joining all the pieces together, like a puzzle, into a kind of picture of Aunt Cass.

When it seemed as if no one had anything else to say, my mother stood up. "Now Patience will sing 'The Riddle Song,'" she said.

I glanced around, wondering which of the old women was Patience.

The voice that broke the silence came from the chair next to mine. It was Pat Hargreaves who sang the song—sang it in a high, clear voice with her eyes shut tight.

> *I gave my love a cherry without a stone.*
> *I gave my love a chicken without a bone.*
> *I gave my love a ring without an end.*
> *I gave my love a baby with no crying.*

As she sang the other verses, I thought about what a riddle Aunt Cass had been. All along, she who had seemed so lighthearted, playing silly tricks on me, was also the serious woman everyone else had talked about. It didn't surprise me that she had liked this song, with its words so full of tricks, its melody so simple and beautiful. It suited her.

At the end of the song, my mother began to thank everyone on behalf of Aunt Cass's family.

"Wait!" I jumped to my feet. "I want to say something, too."

With a look of surprise, Mom sat down again.

I cleared my throat nervously. "I . . . I didn't

know Aunt Cass as long as the rest of you," I said. "But I was probably the last person she helped in a big way. She did something for me that I needed more than anything. She helped me feel at home in a strange place. And..."—I paused, took a deep breath, and went on—"and she also short-sheeted me. Twice."

As I sat down, there was a murmur of quiet laughter.

I felt a touch on my shoulder. It was Pat, who gave me a quick, shy glance, then stared down at the floor.

"Please don't tell the other kids about my name. They'd only make fun of it," she whispered.

"I won't tell anybody. And," I added awkwardly, "the song was good."

"It was Aunt Cass's favorite. I used to sing it to—h-her." She started sobbing, and the Hargreaveses took her away.

My parents and I made our way through the people, stopping many times for Mom to greet old friends and introduce Dad and me. Finally we reached our car, only to be stopped by Judge Bank.

"Sandra, I know this is not the proper time or place to talk, but you should know that Cass made a will some time ago that left Penncroft Farm to this fellow with a bee in his bonnet about immortalizing his ancestors. He might try to take possession soon if you don't come up with that last will—the one Cass put in that hidey-hole of hers."

Dad shook his head. "That Cass—always did love a good riddle, and now she's left us with a pip."

"According to what she said . . . on Halloween," my mother said, clearing her voice and trying not to cry, "anybody with the right spirit can find it. I guess we'll just have to summon up the right spirit," she quavered.

Judge Bank hugged Mom and shook hands with Dad and me, then unlocked the door of his antique car. Ordinarily I would have begged for a chance to get a close look at a Model T, but not that day. There was an important riddle to solve first.

7

Pasty Treats and Hasty Retreats

I ended up that long, sad day sprawled on my bed trying to decipher the dotted lines and colored squares on my history book's map of the Battle of Brandywine. "Chadd's Ford, Jeffries' Ford, Jones's Ford, Brinton's Ford," I read to myself, feeling very confused. "Sounds like a bunch of car dealers." I snapped the book shut and lobbed it to the other end of my bed. As I looked up, my eye was caught by the portrait of my ancestor. I went over for a closer look. "You must have been around during the Revolution," I said aloud. "Wish you could fill me in on Brandywine and what happened with all those darned fords."

I turned to the Pennsylvania map Mom had put on my wall and examined it closely, hoping to find a clue. Chadd's Ford was there, a little town next to Brandywine Creek, but the black line of Route 1, the highway crossing the creek nearby, didn't show a ford or ferry or anything other than a plain old bridge.

I threw myself down on the window seat. My rear came down hard on something knobby. "Ouch!" I said loudly, discovering a metal hinge. Curving my fingers around the edge of the seat, I gave a hard pull. The top flew up, slamming into my nose, which started to bleed. Pinching my nostrils with one hand, I stuck my other inside the hollow base and felt a box—a box big enough to hold a will. My heart thumping, I lifted out the box and gingerly opened it. There was nothing inside but a black leather flower. Disappointment made me throw it down and growl, "Looks like I got a bloody nose for nothing."

"*Nothing*, Lars? That's the cockade of my brother, Will!" It was Geordie, lounging on my bed, buckled shoes and all. "He wore it on his hat. The color showed he sided with Washington. Why, that cockade was Will's only uniform for a good long while."

"Wait a minute," I protested. "What about his

blue-and-tan uniform like George Washington's?" I found my history book and opened it to a picture of Washington.

Geordie sprang up from the bed. "Your ignorance is vastly amusing, Lars. Early in the war, hardly anybody had a real uniform—except for rich people like Washington. And those uniforms were all different colors, not just blue and buff. Some American uniforms were as red as the ones the British soldiers wore." He looked at the history book picture and chuckled. "Nay, country boys like Will were lucky if they had a whole pair of ordinary breeches, let alone a whole uniform. Sometimes they'd make themselves leather hunting shirts to use for a sort of uniform. In truth, Washington liked to have them wear those shirts, because the British figured everybody in one was a genuine sharpshooter. Most of those American boys couldn't hit the broad side of a barn, but they surely did look the part!

"Will was proud of this cockade," Geordie went on, stooping over to pick it up. "Many didn't even have these. Why, when the army marched through Philadelphia, General Washington ordered all the men to put green leaves in their hats so there'd be at least one thing uniform about the troops. 'Twas just before the battle at Brandywine Creek."

"Brandywine!" I crowed. "Great—I was just wishing old George there could talk and help me with this." I waved the Brandywine study sheet at him. "Guess I've been studying too hard. I'm talking to pictures as well as ghos—that is, shades."

"Indeed," Geordie remarked dryly. "I'll tell you about that terrible day, but only if you stay mum. Badger me with questions and I'll not go on. 'Tis a bargain?"

"'Tis," I echoed, barely knowing what I'd bargained for.

That fall of 1777, after Will left home, was probably no stormier than any other, but I remember it as a blustery, tempestuous time. Doubtless my memory is clouded by my father's fury and my mother's despair over Will's joining the patriot forces. As time passed, Father's anger settled down into a sadness that changed him. Before, there had been songs and playful tricks to lighten the tedium of fruit picking. But that fall there was no Will taking away my ladder to strand me on a limb, and no Will's whistle summoning me to cool off in the pond when Father was not about. No, that fall there were but three of us filling our shoulder-hung buckets, our hearts aching as much as our arms.

One September evening, as Mother was making apple butter and I was stringing fruit for drying, Father came storming into the kitchen. "Another folly of those rebel hotheads," he exclaimed bitterly. "And this one's likely to ruin us!"

Quietly, Mother put down her paddle and swung the kettle out away from the coals. Then she moved across to Father. "Seat thyself, Laban, and try for a bit of composure," she said softly.

"Composure? And what composure do they show, those madmen calling themselves the Continental Congress? A congress of traitors, I say. Madmen and traitors!"

I swallowed. "What did the Continental Congress do, Father?"

"That so-called Congress has officially decreed that apples can no longer be exported to England. Our half-picked crop—now worthless! We might as well feed it all to the pigs!"

"Nay, Laban, don't take on so. Surely Geordie can sell the apples in Philadelphia or peddle them to the country inns." Mother passed her hand over his dark hair affectionately.

Father's expression softened. He looked at me and smiled. "Poor Geordie. Seems only yesterday you were playing with gewgaws. Remember the toy soldier from England that I bought in Philadelphia when you were still in leading strings?"

I nodded. Next to the cup and ball that Will had carved of apple wood from our trees, that lead soldier had been my favorite toy. How Mother had protested when Father had given the small grenadier to me! With her Quaker beliefs, she didn't think it fit for child's play.

I also remembered Father's present for Will that same day. The day our first apple shipment to England (arranged by Benjamin Franklin himself) had occasioned a special treat. Father had brought Will a signet ring inscribed grandly in Latin with our family joke about Will's stubbornness and name: "Ubi Voluntas Via Ibi Est" ("Where there's a will, there's a way"). I wrenched myself back to the present and replied to my father's question.

"Aye, I remember the soldier well and still keep it by me, Father. 'Tis my lucky piece. I tried to get Will to take it with him, but perhaps his ring will bring him the luck he needs." I crossed to the settle and took out another length of thread.

When I turned back, the shuttered look had

returned to my father's face. "What Will needs is a dose of reason. I forbid you to mention his name again," he said gruffly.

Mother and I exchanged unhappy looks.

Father began pacing back and forth. "You're right, Patience," he said after a time. "Geordie must peddle those apples, and he'd best start tomorrow. 'Tis rumored the British army is coming up from Chesapeake Bay to take Philadelphia back from the rebels. I for one will give General Howe a most warm welcome—and there are many who share my sentiments, although they've feared to speak out whilst the rebels are in the saddle hereabouts." He crossed the room and opened the cupboard hidden in the woodwork over the fireplace. Inside we kept our spices, money, and valuable papers safe from mildew and robbers.

Father brought out some farthings and closed the cupboard door. "Here's a bit of money for your journey, lad, but try to barter for your board and keep as you go. Gold coins are scarce."

"But, Laban, if the British army is coming, mightn't Geordie be in danger?" Mother protested, her eyes dark with worry.

"Nonsense, Patience. The British are gentlemen, and Geordie is loyal to his king and country. They'll not harm him."

So it was that early the next day I set off with a wagonload of apples, pears, cider, and perry to sell to the country taverns down Brandywine Creek way.

By late afternoon I had sold everything but four kegs of perry. I found a buyer for three of these in Mr. Welsh, whose tavern stood four miles west of Chadd's Ford, one of several places where Brandywine Creek could be waded in safety. These fords, besides being shallow spots in the stream, offered the only clear access to the riverbank, which elsewhere was steep and thickly wooded.

As it was dark by the time I made my bargain with Mr. Welsh, I decided to stay the night. There were few guests, so I had the luxury of a bed to myself. I quickly readied for sleep, rubbing my teeth with a chalked rag and adjusting the bed ropes more tautly under the sagging mattress so that I might sleep tight.

I slept far too tight, not waking until nearly nine. Fearing that Father would be angry at my dawdling, I hurried downstairs to settle up my accounts with the jovial tavern keeper.

Mr. Welsh was busy in the common room with a lively group of customers; he told me they were a patrol of American mounted sentries, called vedettes. *The sight of these Continentals, washing down slabs* of ham with hot, steaming toddy, filled me with great dismay. Last I had heard, the American army was miles away—close to Philadelphia, capital city of the rebellion simply because the Congress of "madmen and traitors" met there. Or had, before fleeing to York. At any rate, the presence of Washington's forces at Welsh's Tavern could mean trouble was close at hand.

I sat down quietly on the puncheon bench and helped myself to the ham. I reckoned I should find out what was going on, else I might blunder into trouble on my way home.

My attention was drawn by the thunderous sound of Mr. Welsh's huge hand slamming down on the rough wooden tabletop. "So, lads, you think I should run and hide like a rabbit because the British are on the way? Nay, I'm a neutral party. I shall pour punch for any thirsty man with nary a thought for his politics!"

One of the soldiers shook his head in disbelief. "But politics is nothing when a battle's in the offing, you fool! A cannonball doesn't stop to inquire if you've taken sides! The British camped last night at Kennett Square, only two miles west of here. They may arrive at any time, going east to Chadd's Ford. But Washington's troops are waiting for them there."

Mr. Welsh took a long swig from his own mug and set it down with a clatter. "If you're so all-fired certain the lobsterbacks are coming through here, you'd best pay your shot and move along. I'd hate for you to be interrupted before settling up."

"It won't be so soon as all that, old man," laughed another vedette. "Pour another round. This day promises to be long and hard, and I must needs fortify myself to face those redcoats."

"I'll settle up with ye now, if you please, sir," I said timidly.

Mr. Welsh's hearty laugh rang out. "Only one gentleman is wise enough to settle his accounts ahead of the lobsterbacks, and 'tis my misfortune to owe him, not the other way round." He slapped me on the back; 'twas kindly meant, but I felt it to my ribs. "You go out and harness your team. When you return, I'll have your money ready for you—and a nunchion to take along."

I thanked the tavern keeper, then ran outside and hitched up my father's slugfooted team, Daisy and Buttercup. A morning fog was rising, but I could clearly see the vedettes' horses tied nearby. When I returned to the common room, Mr. Welsh handed me a small leather pouch full of coins and a bundle that smelt of spicy apple tart and savory beef pasty.

It was then that we heard the first shouts and the sound of marching feet coming up the road from Kennett Square. Instantly, the vedettes dropped to the floor. One crawled like a crayfish across the uneven wooden planks to peek through the shutters. Mr. Welsh and I stood, staring at each other.

"Ready your muskets," hissed the soldier at the window.

Mr. Welsh whispered so loud I thought the pewter tankards would shake on the boards. "Nay! Don't fire! There are too many. You'll rot in prison ships or in the grave unless you get out!"

"But we can't reach our horses!"

"Then use your bloody feet!" Mr. Welsh growled. "Take the path at the back. It comes out down the road closer to Chadd's."

The men rushed from the room. Petrified with fear, I watched Mr. Welsh stride across and throw open the front door. I could hear his voice booming forth. "Welcome to Welsh's Tavern, sir. May I offer you a hot toddy to ward off this dreary fog? Geordie, be a good lad and fetch a mugful for this officer."

My hands were shaking so that I could barely keep the toddy from sloshing over the edges of the cup, but somehow I managed to heat the drink with a red-hot poker and carry it outside without spilling too much. Out of the corner of my eye, I glimpsed red-coated soldiers in endless columns, but fear kept my gaze to the ground as I approached the officer.

A rolling laugh brought my eyes up. This officer was no lobsterback; indeed, his coat was as blue as Washington's, though he wore a red-and-silver sash and his cockade was edged with gold. I figured he must be one of the German soldiers hired to fight for the British—one of the Hessians so hated by the patriots. To me, his round face looked like that of one of the German farmers I'd seen selling vegetables at the High Street Market in Philadelphia.

"Ja, is dusty for all the fog is damp," he said. He raised the mug and drank thirstily.

Mr. Welsh asked, most politely, who was commanding the column. The officer answered, "Knyphausen." This outlandish name tickled my fancy, and, despite my state of terror—or perhaps because of it—nervous laughter bubbled up inside me.

"Vat is so funny, young man?" the officer asked sternly.

"Oh, sir, I . . . I . . . ," I gasped.

"The lad is but a simpleton—a witling, sir," said Mr. Welsh hastily, pointing significantly to his head.

"I fear this war has addled his wits even further. I pray you let him depart in peace. His is that old rig yonder."

The Hessian officer looked at my team and wagon, then peered at me. I let my jaw hang slack and goggled at him blankly.

"We don't make war on Idioten, and we don't need those broken-down creatures. Someone has left us better horseflesh. Friends of yours?" he challenged Mr. Welsh.

The tavern keeper's laugh rang out. "Mine, sir? And me loyal to the core—as is this poor boy's father. Run along home now, Geordie. Now, Geordie." Once again that huge hand landed on my back, this time propelling me smartly in the direction of my rig. I leaped into the seat and drove away, for the first time grateful that Daisy and Buttercup were slow as molasses. Had they looked fleeter-footed, the British likely would have confiscated them along with the horses of the luckless Continental patrol.

Since the British columns blocked the road going west, I was forced to turn east, toward Chadd's Ford. Soon I came in sight of Kennett Meetinghouse. I could see that the Friends were assembled for mid-week meeting, and I stopped to warn them that the

British were not far behind me. What a waste of precious time! They thanked me for the warning but went calmly on with their meeting as if I had never interrupted, even though shots were now ringing out behind me on the road.

I hunkered down on the seat and looked desperately about for a place to turn off the main road. To my great relief, I found a lane that headed north. It was barely more than wheel ruts in the dirt, but at least 'twas clear of trees—and soldiers. Seemingly oblivious to my fears, Daisy and Buttercup ambled along at their regular snail's pace, despite my shaking the reins to urge them faster. Such effort only delayed me further, for one of the reins snapped. It took the better part of an hour to mend. Thus, it was past noon before I reached Street Road and turned east toward Jones's Ford, several miles upstream from Chadd's Ford, where the Americans were waiting for the British attack.

Crossing at Jones's Ford was not easy—I had to pick my way around felled logs in the stream, and an American patrol stopped me on the east side for questioning. When I said I'd seen troops at Welsh's but none since, the captain nodded. "Just what Major Spear reported. I don't know what that blind fool

Colonel Bland saw going up to the fork, but it surely wasn't redcoats! Now you'd best get along, boy," he said.

Mystified, I got along. Then, toiling up a steep slope, I heard rolling, distant thunder. I looked at the sky. It was cloudless—even the morning fog had burned away under the bright, hot sun. Again the rumbling rent the air, and this time I knew 'twas no thunderclap but the firing of guns, louder than I'd ever heard. I stopped the wagon to listen closely, trying to decide where the ominous sound was coming from. Panic rose in my chest until I could scarcely catch my breath. Instinctively, I reached into my pocket and brought out my lucky piece. The small lead grenadier in the red-painted tunic stood on my palm, aiming down his long musket. Clutching the toy, I made a childish wish that it could tell me what to do.

But a much larger and less silent figure decided my course of action. I heard a peculiar muttering in the woods nearby—a string of oaths. Without stopping to think, I raised up my lead soldier to throw at the mutterer. Then I saw his face: It belonged to Squire Thomas Cheyney, a swarthy, thickset man who had been a friend of my father's before the war had set them at odds. As the squire thrashed his way through the bushes with his riding crop, he scowled and swore like a madman. When he spotted me, his mouth opened into a perfect O of astonishment.

"Why, Geordie, what are you doing here?" he gasped.

"Been delivering perry at Welsh's."

"Then your horses are fresh?" he inquired eagerly.

"If you want to call them that. Slowest nags in creation."

"At least they're not lame," he said with disgust. "I had to leave my infernal mount tied to a stile and was nearly caught by the redcoats! Give me a hand up, lad. We must hurry."

"What do you mean?" I asked, helping him up beside me.

"Why, we must warn Washington about this flanking action!"

"Flanking action?" I echoed, still not understanding.

"Aye. Ten thousand British are crossing the two branches of the Brandywine north of the fork, guided by the Tory Galloway. I saw them myself! They'll come down Birmingham Road behind the American line and fall upon the Continentals from the rear. And by the cannon fire coming from the south, I judge Howe has sent some troops to make Washington believe that that is where the main attack will come."

"Aye, troops under Knyphausen are moving against Chadd's."

Cheyney pounded his fist down on the seat. "I thought so! 'Tis the same trick Howe used to win at Long Island! I tried to warn General Sullivan of this, but he thought I was exaggerating! Well, at least the damned fool gave me a pass to Washington's headquarters. I'll need your wagon."

My expression must have resembled one of the idiots the Hessian thought me to be, for the squire said, more kindly, "If you're too feared to come, wait here for me. I'll be back as soon as I can."

"Father will flay me if I help the Continentals, but..." Suddenly I thought of my brother, Will. I couldn't let him be taken by surprise. "Aye, I'm going with you!" I blurted out.

"That's a brave lad!" the squire cried. He seized the reins and whipped up the horses until they ran as if wolves were nipping at their hooves.

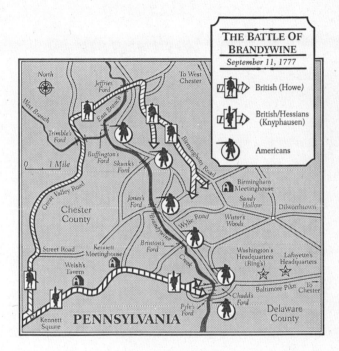

THE BATTLE OF BRANDYWINE
September 11, 1777

British (Howe)

British/Hessians (Knyphausen)

Americans

North

West Branch

Trimble's Ford

Jeffrie's Ford

East Branch

To West Chester

Buffington's Ford

Skunk's Ford

Birmingham Road

Birmingham Meetinghouse

Sandy Hollow

Dilworthtown

0   1 Mile

Great Valley Road

Chester County

Jones's Ford

Wistar's Woods

Wylie Road

Brandywine Creek

Street Road

Kennett Meetinghouse

Brinton's Ford

Welsh's Tavern

Washington's Headquarters (Ring's)

Lafayette's Headquarters

Baltimore Pike

To Chester

Kennett Square

Pyle's Ford

Chadd's Ford

Delaware County

PENNSYLVANIA

8

A Warning for Washington

As it turned out, Squire Cheyney and I didn't get far before the road along the creek grew too crowded with American troops for our wagon to pass. Nothing daunted, Cheyney said we must leave the wagon on Wylie Road and ride the three miles overland to Ring's house, Washington's headquarters near Chadd's Ford. With growing misgivings, I helped unhitch the team and conceal the wagon in the woods, and soon we were up on Daisy's and Buttercup's bare backs, trotting over the rough ground. I clutched Buttercup's reins and mane for dear life as I followed Squire Cheyney up and down the steep wooded hills, more than once nearly sliding backward off Buttercup's rump or forward over his head. Cheyney, all unheeding, allowed branches to whip behind him into my face; they stung like the very devil.

As we came out of the trees on the hill behind Ring's house and paused to get our bearings, I quickly forgot my stinging face, for I could hear the sharp staccato of musketry coming from Brandywine Creek below. The thought that Will might be the target made me sick with fear.

Cheyney glanced at me. "Never heard muskets before, boy?" he asked brusquely, gathering up his reins.

I shuddered. "Not trained on men. And not when one of those men might be my brother, and he could be shot from the back."

"We'll prevent that if we get through in time! And Ring's is just below!" the squire cried, goading the winded Daisy into a gallop down the hill. As we reached the stone wall behind Washington's head-quarters, a line of Continentals blocked our way. One grabbed Daisy's bridle and barked, "Don't you know there's a battle brewing? This is no place for farmers!"

"Don't be daft, sir!" Cheyney roared. "We've a pass from Sullivan to deliver urgent information to General Washington."

He held out a piece of paper. After the guard read it, he quickly motioned us on. Cheyney chirruped his horse down the hill, with mine wheezing along behind. We stopped beside the well. Dismounting, the squire sprinted around the side of the house and I scuttled behind him to the wide front door.

Two brawny sentries brought us both to a halt. Squire Cheyney, glaring at them, simply hallooed through the doorway in a voice Knyphausen likely could hear above the booming cannon beyond the Brandywine. I caught my breath, not only because my brother's life hung in the balance, but also because I was to see the man many revered as a god— and my father reviled as the devil.

My suspense lasted but a trice. A dignified figure in a buff-and-blue uniform appeared before us— General Washington.

Broad-shouldered, taller than anyone I'd ever seen, he regarded us through icy blue eyes. "There had better be an excellent reason for this interruption, sir," he exclaimed.

After all his sprinting and bellowing, Cheyney had little breath for speech. He panted like a landed fish for several long moments. Then, finally, he gasped out, "'Tis the British, ten thousand strong, crossing upstream to attack from behind."

Washington narrowed his eyes, looked us over as if we stank of barn muck, and motioned us into the house.

"I heard some such nonsense from Colonel Bland, but later reports proved this false," he said, frowning. "Local sources have assured me there is no ford above the fork that's close enough to offer a serious threat. No, it's here at Chadd's Ford that the British attack will come, and here at the Brandywine is where we'll hold them!" In an undertone, he added, "Indeed we must: No other obstacles lie 'twixt Howe and Philadelphia save the Schuylkill River—at the very doors of the city!"

The squire could barely contain his outrage. "Local sources be damned!" he spluttered. "I am a local source. And a local source most loyal to your efforts! Don't you know that most of the farmers who've stayed nearby, in Howe's path, are neutrals or Tories who want to throw dust in your eyes?" His voice squeaked with fury, and with despair I perceived that he sounded too much like a bedlamite to be taken seriously.

Washington dismissed Cheyney's words with a wave of his hand. "And why should I not think you are doing the same? Nay, I choose to believe the word of an innocent youth before that of a man puffed full of Tory guile!"

"Tory guile?!" Cheyney squawked, as ruffled as a fighting cock.

"Yes, an innocent such as this lad here."

Suddenly I felt pride and glory swelling within me. As puffed up as any guileful man, I stepped forward and gazed up expectantly at that lofty, grave countenance.

"Aye, this lad," repeated Washington. "Now confound the boy, where'd he get to?...Ned—Ned Owens?"

"Here, Excellency." As we stood in the corridor, I could see a pudgy boy standing at a sideboard in the room to the right. In one hand he held a meat pasty; in the other, a pewter tankard. Juice from one or the other was dribbling down his cheeks. Crestfallen, I watched him wipe his mouth on his sleeve.

"Have you heard what this man says, Owens?"

"Aye, sir. And it be lies. I've been up and down the Brandywine—all the way north to the fork—and there's nary a ford you've not covered with patrols." He leveled a look at me that was brimming over with self-importance. 'Twas this barefaced conceit that gave me back my tongue.

"But the British crossed above the fork, at Jeffries' Ford!" I exclaimed. "The squire saw them, and I know him to be true to the patriot cause. Redcoats in the thousands will be coming south down Birmingham Road, behind you to the east! Don't let them flank your troops, sir. My brother, Will, is a Continental, and I couldn't bear..."

I shall never know why—'twas probably a storm of nerves after all I'd been through and my fears for Will—but then and there I burst into tears. No man would have done so, but 'tis likely my sobs did more than any man's vows (and surely more than Cheyney's dismayed howls) to convince Washington of the truth.

For a long moment those cool blue eyes took my measure. Just then an aide dashed into the room and thrust some papers into Washington's hand. From what he said, it appeared they were reports verifying all that Squire Cheyney and I had told the general. Washington immediately ordered word sent to Sullivan to meet the column advancing on his rear. After the aide's departure, the general buckled on his sword. As he did so, he asked, "What's your name, lad?"

"Geordie."

"We need drummer boys, Geordie. Join us, as Owens here has done." He threw these words over his shoulder as he strode from the room. Jealously, I glanced at Owens. How much I wanted to take up the drum—and how impossible that I do so!

Squire Cheyney cleared his throat. "Well done, Geordie." He mopped his brow with a handkerchief. "We'd best head back north to Wylie Road. 'Twill be safe enough—the main battle will surely be to the east, where the redcoats are."

We hurried outside, but before we could mount, one of Washington's aides sped up the path and stopped the squire.

"Go along with the courier and show Sullivan the way to Birmingham Road!" He cast a disparaging look at Daisy. "That nag will not be quick enough. Come, I'll find another for you."

Squire Cheyney handed me Daisy's reins with a warning to waste no time, then rushed away with the aide. By this time the gunfire was quickening, making Buttercup as skittish as an unbroken filly. I was still trying to get up on her when General Washington himself emerged from the house, calling for a guide to lead him to Birmingham Road.

I half hoped and half feared that I would be that guide, but instead his aides brought up an elderly man from the neighborhood, Mr. Joseph Brown. Old Mr. Brown made every possible excuse not to go, but in the end was convinced at swordpoint where his duty lay. When he protested his lack of a horse, one of Washington's aides dismounted from his own fine charger.

As Brown reluctantly climbed into the saddle, Washington sat impatiently on his own beautiful white horse. The instant the frightened farmer was in place, Washington snapped a whip at the rump of the reluctant guide's horse, which leaped into a gallop. The general followed, spurring his own mount until its nose pushed into the leader's flank like a colt suckling its mother. Even this didn't satisfy Washington, who cracked his whip and shouted, "Push along, old man, push along!" Spellbound, I watched the two race up the hill across the golden fields, jumping the fences as they came to them. I had never seen such horsemanship—superb on the part of the general, dreadful on the part of Mr. Brown. Behind them ran a ragged line of soldiers, rucksacks bobbing as they sped over the uneven ground.

After the two mismatched leaders disappeared over the brow of the hill, I managed to get on Buttercup and take hold of Daisy's bridle. It took very little urging to hasten the two frightened horses north, away from the sound of gunfire. By the time I got back to my wagon, my hands were too shaky for my fingers to work properly, and it took ages to harness the team. At the very moment I climbed to the seat and took up the reins, the valley behind me exploded with artillery fire. Terrified, Daisy and Buttercup reared in their traces. Up and up they went, pawing the smoke-filled air. Then they plunged back to the *ground, landing at a dead run. For a few breathless moments I simply clung to the reins, pulling for all I was worth, but the horses were too panic-stricken to feel the bits sawing at their mouths. My arms ached from the effort, and I eased off to recover some strength for another try.* Perhaps my horses bolting might be a blessing in disguise, *I thought. It would surely get me away from the Brandywine much faster than their usual pace. Then I realized where we were headed: due east toward Birmingham Road, where the British and Americans were about to clash in battle.*

With strength born of fear, I reached for the brake, only to have the lever break off in my hand. Clutching the reins, I shut my eyes and prayed. At the sound of gunfire, my eyes flew open once more. Up the hill to my left were two lines of soldiers. At the top of the ridge, one line raised their muskets in unconscious mimicry of the toy soldier in my pocket. Their tall caps were as pointed as my little grenadier's, their tunics as scarlet. But my toy had never spat forth puffs of smoke or blazes of fire as did the muzzles glinting in the sun. My eyes shifted down to the target below: the second line of soldiers, whose black cockaded hats proclaimed them Continentals. Under my horrified gaze, this American line wavered and broke, some few soldiers staying to return fire, but most wheeling in confusion toward the road down which my team was bolting.

As the wagon careened down the dusty lane, I glimpsed still, crumpled figures, their coats turning red with blood, lying in the field where the American line had stood. The thought that Will might be bleeding to death under the hot September sun made me steer my winded team into a thick copse of beech trees to consider what to do. 'Twas lucky I did, else I'd never have heard it—the faint but unmistakable sound of Will's whistle. I shook my head, thinking I must be imagining things. Then it came again more clearly from the thicket ahead.

I shot off the wagon seat and hurtled into the woods, crashing through underbrush in the manner of an animal fleeing a forest fire. My lips puckered soundlessly in the vain effort to whistle back. "Will! Where are you?" I finally called hoarsely.

Through the leaves, a gleam of pallid skin told me I'd found him. Will lay at the base of a beech tree looking much as he did napping in our orchard after a dip in our pond on a hot summer day. But the dark red daubs on his leg came from no pond.

"Geordie! I thought my eyes were playing tricks on me, seeing you pull up in our wagon. But when I whistled and you looked startled as a deer, I knew 'twas really you. Trust you to be in Wistar's Woods just when things got hot." Managing a feeble grin, he tried to sit up. Then his face contorted with pain, and he fell back with a groan that tore at my heart.

"Don't you worry, Will," I said with a confidence I was far from feeling. "I'm taking you home."

"Nay," Will said weakly. "If the lobsterbacks catch you..."

"Hush, you great booby. I still have some perry in the wagons; I can bribe my way through the whole British army with you safely hidden under the hay. You look as if you could use a cupful." I ran to the wagon and fetched a tin cup full of perry for him. Will's hands shook so much I had to help him hold the cup, but the strong cider appeared to strengthen him a little.

With every moment, the sounds of battle crept closer. In my distraction, I noticed that golden leaves were sifting down upon us, but it was early for the trees to be shedding so much of their foliage. An odd buzzing sound drew my attention. I looked up and saw the cause of the early autumn: deadly grapeshot whizzing back and forth through the trees cutting down the leaves as it had cut down the young men in the field.

Frantically I ripped off my shirt and tore it in two. As gently as I could, I wrapped one half around Will's wounded leg. It was agony for both of us, but I had to staunch the bleeding, else he'd die before I even got him into the wagon. If I could get him that far. He was at least a foot taller than I, and heavier by several stone. Without daring to think of the impossibility of my task, I knotted the other piece of shirt round Will's wrists, slipped them over my head, and started to crawl for the wagon, dragging my brother beneath me. He cried out so piteously that I froze, but a burst of artillery fire shook the earth beneath me and I lunged forward convulsively. I don't know if Will struck his head or fainted, but suddenly he went slack, his deadweight bringing me down on top of him so abruptly that my face hit the ground. Everything swirled in a dizzy spiral.

It was the blood streaming down my own face that spurred me back into action. I clawed wildly to lift myself enough to give Will air. Then, slowly we inched forward to the wagon, stopped behind it, and I gently eased my head out from Will's hands. Leaving him below, I jumped up on the wagon and fixed the slats down at their loading angle. Grabbing the rope of the loading pulley, I tied it to Will's wrists and grasped the other end. Though I strained and heaved with every ounce of strength I possessed, I couldn't budge him.

Will's eyes flickered open and he moaned.

"Will," I cried. "Can you crawl any? I can't pull you..."

But Will fell back senseless once more.

I was in such despair that I didn't hear anyone approaching until I saw him standing next to me—a man in a scarlet jacket with little wings on the shoulders and a tall helmet of black fur. Even without it, he was the tallest man I'd ever seen, that British grenadier.

Without a word, we stared at each other. Then he drew one arm over his face to wipe the sweat out of his eyes. I didn't move, though I could feel the blood dripping down my own face and the sting of the sweat running into the cuts on my cheek.

His eyes flicked over me and then down to Will and the telltale cockade on his hat.

"My brother," I said, and opened my palms to him in appeal.

Still silent, the grenadier set down his musket and swung the pack off his back to the ground with a loud thud that showed how very heavy it was. Then he gathered Will up in his arms and carefully laid him down upon the wagon bed.

"Be that drink?" he asked, jutting his chin toward the barrel of perry.

I nodded my head, speechless.

"I could use a bit o' drink. Seventeen miles I've marched since dawn. Seventeen miles in all this heat. 'Tis enough to kill a man, even without the efforts of this lot." He jerked his thumb at Will.

I swarmed up the slats, filled a cup, and thrust it at him. The soldier drained it in one gulp and held the cup out for more. I hastily obliged. After downing the second cupful, he picked up his pack and musket.

"Thankee, lad," he growled, and plunged back into the woods before I could thank him in return.

I had no time to ponder what had happened. The sounds of muskets were all around me in the woods, and the next redcoat to come upon us might not be so helpful. Quickly, I replaced the slats across the wagon and flung myself back on the seat. Even in my hurry, I felt an uncomfortable lump under my breeches.

It was my lead soldier. I took it up in my hand and gazed at it. After the flesh-and-blood grenadiers I'd seen in the field and in the forest, the toy seemed different. With all the force that remained to me, I threw it down to the ground and left it behind me on the Brandywine battlefield.

I turned southeast past Sandy Hollow, joining a trickle of Continentals fleeing toward Dilworthtown. I slaked their thirst with the perry, while it lasted. The poor fellows deserved it.

It was midnight by the time we came up our lane. By great good fortune my father, exhausted by his harvest work, was sleeping too soundly to hear us arrive, but my mother's ear was sharpened with worry. She soon rushed out of the house, lantern in hand. As she stood there, the wind swirled her long white shift about her ankles and sent her long brown hair, loosened for bed, flying about her head.

"Geordie, I thought thee'd never get home!" she cried when she saw me.

"There was a battle at Brandywine, Mother. I found..."

"Geordie, thee knows I don't believe in bloodshed...no matter what the cause," she cut in. "It's bad enough to have thy brother run away and break thy father's heart, but now thee, too..." Her voice faltered as she followed my mute gesture toward the wagon bed. "It's Will! Oh, Geordie, he isn't dead?"

"No, but grievously wounded."

Mother felt Will's forehead, then quickly looked over his wounds, murmuring under her breath all the while. "Ever since Will ran away, thy father has said he would treat him like the traitor he is should he return. I must think what's best to do." She pressed her hands to her head as if that would untangle her thoughts. Then, with an air of decision, she told me we would hide Will in Grampa's Folly.

This was a secret room my grandfather had insisted Father build into the barn foundation. Grampa had a fear of Indian raids and wanted a refuge handy in case of attack. Of course, there had never been any Indian raids—in fact, the only raids I heard about were the other way around. The Indians in our part of the colony had always been peaceful farmers. Indeed, they had taught the settlers the best ways to till the soil.

Now, however, we were heartily glad of Grandfather's stubbornness. The two of us managed to get Will to the barn, open the hidden door, and put him down on a pile of straw.

Will's eyes fluttered open. "Water," he murmured, then his eyelids closed once more.

Mother and I looked at each other, jubilant at this proof that he still lived. I ran for the spring, she for the herb garden to gather lamb's-ear leaves to bandage and soothe his wounds.

It was not easy over the next few weeks to care for Will and keep Father ignorant of his presence in the barn. During that time I confided to my gentle Quaker mother the tale of how I had come to find Will in the beech grove. Though horror-struck by the dangers I had run and the sights I had seen, she conceded that my action had surely saved my brother's life.

Reports sifted in about the outcome of the Brandywine battle that had engulfed me and wounded Will. I heard that the American divisions, lacking the training to wheel and face the redcoats coming up behind them, had ended up dangerously separated from each other. Attempts to close the gap resulted in even more confusion—so much so that some Continentals had even fired on their own advance lines. As for the men pelting across the fields behind Washington and Mr. Brown, they had fought valiantly, but finally had had to retreat in disarray.

Still, 'twas said that Washington's men were not downcast by their defeat, especially since the British were too exhausted by their long day's march to pursue them. For a fortnight after Brandywine, the Continentals had done their best to keep Howe from crossing the Schuylkill, but to no avail. By late September, the British occupied Philadelphia.

Father was delighted, but Mother and I scarcely cared about the capture of the capital (if it could be called such after Congress had fled), for Will was safe at home again.

9

Battlefield
Field Trip

When my alarm went off the next morning, I realized I hadn't filled in my Brandywine study sheet. Geordie and I had been interrupted by Dad, who thumped on the wall and told me to stop muttering and get to sleep. His orders couldn't have come at a worse time. After Geordie had finished telling me of his Brandywine ventures, I had asked him about the secret room in the barn, where they had hidden Will.

"I haven't seen anything like that—what did you call it?—Grampa's Folly," I'd said. "I guess it must have been in the part that burned. Right?"

Geordie had looked at me intently before replying, "What a nimble wit you have, Lars. However did you figure that out?"

"Oh, it was easy enough. There's obviously no secret room in the part that's left," I'd answered.

"*Obviously* not...," Geordie had started to say, but the rest of his reply was forestalled by my father's pounding.

Now, as I hastily filled in the blanks on the Brandywine paper, I thought the questions were so easy that a sapskull could have answered them. That, and a couple of other interesting things, was what Geordie had called me when I'd asked why the British hadn't used the bridge across the Brandywine instead of marching way up to the forks. I'd showed him Route 1 on my wall map.

"Lars, you sapskull, you witling, you great booby! Nary a bridge was built for a score or more years!"

I chuckled at the memory of Geordie's scolding as I scribbled my answers in the blanks. Then I stuffed the sheet into my backpack and clattered downstairs. As I reached the kitchen, the knocker sounded on the front door.

"Who could that be at this hour?" Dad said from behind his newspaper. "Get it, will you, Lars?"

Obediently I went to the door. A balding, pudgy stranger who looked oddly familiar stood there.

"I'm Edward Owens the Ninth," he announced in a pompous way. "Are your parents at home?"

I returned to the kitchen and told my folks who

it was, adding, "I think he's the father of a kid in my class."

After Dad went to see what Mr. Owens wanted, Mom made a face. "I used to know a guy named Owens who lived around here. He was really a pest," she whispered to me.

"If he's anything like his son, I think it's the same guy."

Dad and Mr. Owens came into the kitchen.

My mother stared at the man. "Edward?" she asked.

"Sandra—haven't seen you in years," Mr. Owens said. "I heard you were staying with Cass. Unfortunately, I didn't know about her passing away until too late to get to the funeral. I just came by to offer my condolences."

Mom looked away. "Thank you, Edward," she said softly.

"And . . . to inquire when we might take possession."

Dad said sharply, "Take possession of what?"

"Penncroft Farm. Surely you knew Cass intended to leave it for a museum? She promised it to me . . . oh, a good ten years ago."

My parents looked thunderstruck.

Mr. Owens cleared his throat. "Well, I wanted

to make sure you knew, so you could plan to move out as soon as possible."

"I...I...," Mom gasped.

Dad interceded. "It's far too soon to be talking about this—can't you see we're still grieving for her?"

"Besides," I blurted out, "she made a new will!"

Mr. Owens's eyes flicked over to me.

"Fine," he said dryly. "Then we'll see you in probate court. Sandra, good to see you again. Don't bother—I'll see myself out." He strode from the room.

The three of us sat in shocked silence.

Finally, I spoke up. "Don't worry, Mom, I'll find it."

Mom sighed and ruffled my hair. "I hope you can, Lars, but considering that most of the time you can't even find your own shoes, I'm not too optimistic. Hey, look at that time! I'd better run you to the end of the pike or you'll miss your bus."

I caught the school bus, but just barely. As soon as I got to school, our class climbed onto another bus for a field trip to Brandywine. After an hour's ride, Mrs. Hettrick stood up and clapped her hands for attention.

"Before we go into the park, class, we'll take a

look at Brandywine Creek itself. After all, if it hadn't been for the creek, the battle here might have gone differently."

"Yeah, maybe the Americans would have won," Eddie Owens shouted. Despite my best effort to avoid him, he was sitting right behind me.

"Actually, if it weren't for the creek, the Americans wouldn't have been here—the battle would have been somewhere else," I remarked to no one in particular.

Eddie leaned over my shoulder. "Fat lot you know about it, Lars," he snorted. "You've never even had it in school. You said so yourself."

I made a big thing out of wiping off my shoulder where Eddie had snorted. When I looked up, my eyes met those of Pat Hargreaves, who looked amused at what I'd done. She quickly looked away.

Soon someone pointed out the roadside sign for the village of Chadd's Ford. The name caused a lurch of excitement in my stomach. Chadd's Ford— where the Americans had waited on the east bank of Brandywine Creek for a massive British attack that had never come. I could almost see Knyphausen's Hessian troops lined up on the west side of the stream to draw Washington's attention away from the real attack coming from behind. I could almost hear the cannon booming on the hillside and see the leaves cut down by grapeshot.

Eddie Owens's whining voice broke into my private vision. "Heck, that creek doesn't look like much. Bet I could wade that any day, any place."

Irritated, I turned around. "Not then you couldn't, Owens. The banks were steep and jammed with trees. You couldn't have gotten through, especially with a pack like those British soldiers had to wear."

"Bet I could."

"No way."

Mrs. Hettrick materialized in the aisle beside us. "I think you boys should stop arguing and concentrate on Brandywine," she said with a frown.

From across the aisle, Pat grinned. "That's what they're fighting about. Would you believe it?"

"All right, then, one of you answer this question. Why did the Americans take up positions here at Brandywine Creek?"

"To stop the British from reaching Philadelphia, which was the capital where the Congress was and all," parroted Eddie. Then enthusiasm spurred him on. "And my great-great-great-great-something-grandfather practically turned this battle around. Why, he . . ."

Mrs. Hettrick's eyes seemed to glaze over. "You can tell us all about your illustrious ancestor when we get to the museum, Eddie, but now I want an answer to my question."

I heard a voice answering, and discovered with some surprise that it was my own. "Because this was the main road east from Kennett Square, where the British were camped after marching up from Chesapeake Bay. The Brandywine was the last natural barrier between the British and Philadelphia except for the Schuylkill River, which was at the very doors of the city."

The astonishment on Mrs. Hettrick's face, reflected on those of the kids, made me falter into silence.

"Aren't *you* the Norweirdgian bookworm!" whispered Eddie.

Mrs. Hettrick beamed. "Good work, Lars. I can tell you've been doing some reading. Cass would have been proud of you."

Having so much attention paid to me didn't please Eddie. "Mrs. Hettrick," he said, wildly waving his hand.

"Yes, Eddie?" she sighed.

"Why didn't they just use the bridge? That's what I want to know. I would have just marched my men over that bridge and . . ."

"Owens, you sapskull, you witling, you great booby! No bridge was built for a score or more years," I exclaimed, in an unconscious echo of Geordie.

There was a long moment of silence.

Mrs. Hettrick cleared her throat. "Perhaps you don't know our school rules, Lars. But we don't allow students to use bad words—even unfamiliar ones. I'll let it go this time, but . . ."

"They sure have weird cuss words in Minneapolis," Eddie Owens put in, looking smug at my getting in trouble.

"I didn't learn those words in Minnesota—," I began, then stopped when I realized just where I had learned them.

"I think you've been watching too much 'Monty Python,' Lars," Pat said with a grin. "You're getting a British accent!"

"Yeah. Don't forget the guys who talked like that here at Brandywine were wearing red coats!" Eddie hooted.

"Not necessarily," said Mrs. Hettrick. "Remember, the Americans were mostly British immigrants and their descendants. It was impossible to identify a man's allegiance by his accent. People talked like that on both sides. That was one reason it was so hard to prevent all the spying—and to keep track of those who kept switching loyalties. Now, can anyone tell me why Washington didn't know about the fords upstream?"

I sat through the following pause, determined not to say anything else to embarrass myself. But the pause lengthened until I couldn't stand it anymore.

"Most of the patriots who lived around here left when they heard Howe was coming, and the people who stuck around were either loyalists—who deliberately lied about the fords to Washington—or neutrals, like Mr. Welsh of the tavern nearby. He didn't help either side; he just filled their tankards."

The other students looked at me blankly.

Mrs. Hettrick, intent on getting her main point across to the children, pressed on where I left off. "So, you see, poor Washington never knew what hit him."

I found myself disagreeing aloud with the teacher. "No, Mrs. Hettrick. He *did* have a warning—but it was too late."

"I think you must be mistaken, Lars. I've never heard of any warning. Where did you read about that?"

I shrugged and replied vaguely, "Somewhere. I don't know."

"That's what I've been trying to tell you," squeaked Eddie. "It was my ancestor who..."

"Here we are!" cut in Mrs. Hettrick. "Sorry, Eddie, you'll have to tell us later."

The bus doors opened and the students spilled out. Half the class milled around the parking lot, others started to climb the hill toward the picnic area, and the rest began to move in the general direction of the park museum.

"I feel like General Washington," laughed Mrs. Hettrick. "We both had the same problems here at Brandywine getting our undisciplined troops moving in the right direction at the right time. Just imagine how much more complicated it must have been to get thousands of men where they had to be." She raised her voice and told the stragglers that the class was first to go to the museum and could wander about later.

Once inside, we were able to poke around on our own, looking at the exhibits. Some exhibits explained the finer points of the battle, while others held relics of the soldiers themselves: flesh forks, kettle hooks, shaving gear, and other personal stuff found on the battlefield. Though more excited by each display, I tried to cover up my enthusiasm. I didn't want to be teased about my sudden knowledge, especially when I couldn't give a reasonable explanation for it. I'd already blabbed far too much to feel comfortable.

With a mask of indifference, I followed the group around the museum. Suddenly, Eddie Owens gave a triumphant shout and pointed at one of the display cases. "See, I was right!" he crowed. "My great-great-great-whatever-grandfather *did* warn Washington..."

I joined the flock of students that clustered around Eddie, who oozed smugness.

There under the glass was a photocopy of a letter written by Washington himself. The spidery handwriting was hard to read, but a typewritten version lay next to it. With a pounding heart, I read through the flowery salutation and scanned the rest until I came to a section that seemed to jump off the page at me.

Despite the men's lack of training, the troops acquitted themselves remarkably well on the field of battle

*at Brandywine. It was cursed ill luck that we failed
to learn of the upper fords until so late. If Cheyney
and the boy hadn't come to warn us of the British
flanking action, however, what was a retreat might
have been total destruction. Bless them....*

I looked up from the letter into Eddie Owens's
beaming, chubby face.

"That boy who warned Washington was my ancestor," said Eddie. "My dad is convinced of it. Just
think: George Washington actually knew *my* ancestor...and talked to him right here at Brandywine."

And fed him right here at Brandywine, I thought.
Geordie's description of the boy filching food from
the sideboard at Washington's headquarters flashed
so vividly in my head that for a moment I could almost see the juices running down Eddie's face.

Eddie's ancestor had told General Washington
about the fords on the Brandywine, all right—and
he had told him all wrong. The boy with Squire
Cheyney, I remembered with a quiet glow of pride,
had been Geordie. My friend. My shade. But there
was nothing I could say to set the story straight.

Mrs. Hettrick bustled up, curious at the crowd
around Eddie.

"Lars, I spoke with the museum guide, and he

says you were right: Washington did hear about the flanking, from a Squire Cheyney and a boy who..."

"A boy named Owens, Mrs. Hettrick!" erupted Eddie.

Mrs. Hettrick paused. "No one knows that for sure, Eddie. It might have been some other boy."

"But look at this letter..."

Mrs. Hettrick cut him off firmly. "It doesn't give his name." She turned to me with a pleased expression on her face. "I must say, Lars, you've caught up with us with extraordinary speed. I'll have to send a note to your parents."

Eddie was determined to have his say, however. "But my dad's got all these other letters and stuff proving what my ancestor did. We're going to put them in the new museum at..."

"Oh, shut up, Eddie," said Pat.

I wasn't crazy about being defended by a girl, but I suppose it was better than nothing. At least it worked. Eddie must have remembered Pat's slap.

I moved on to look at the next display of a tall fur hat labeled *British Grenadier's Bearskin Cap.* Then suddenly my eyes focused on a small figure nearly hidden behind a British cartridge box.

It was a leaden toy soldier with a hat molded into a grenadier's cap like the real one beside it and a musket held up in firing position. Most of the figure was a dull metallic gray, but in the creases of the tunic remained a few traces of red paint.

My eyes flew to read the label: *This toy soldier, stamped* London, *was found on the battlefield near Sandy Hollow. It is likely a souvenir of home and family, lost from the pack of a British soldier during the battle.*

My throat felt funny, but I couldn't tell if the cause was laughter or sadness—or both. How could anyone have guessed it had been deliberately thrown away by an American boy?

Mrs. Hettrick clapped her hands. "Okay, group, now we're going to walk over to Lafayette's headquarters. You can stand under the actual sycamore tree where Lafayette lay after being wounded in the leg at Sandy Hollow. But please don't race over there. *We* don't want any wounded this trip!"

Lafayette wasn't the only one with a leg wound from this battle, I thought. Even as I followed the others toward the farmhouse used by Lafayette, my thoughts turned to Will. What had happened after Geordie got his injured brother back to Penncroft Farm?

My eagerness to find out the rest of the story made the day drag by. When I finally got off the bus at Seek-No-Further Pike, I ran all the way to Penn-croft Farm.

My mother was in the kitchen, which looked as if it had been hit by a good old Minnesota tornado. Every cupboard door and drawer was open, with everything pulled out and scattered on the kitchen floor.

"What a mess!" I said, looking around.

Mom rolled her eyes. "I'm glad you're develop-ing standards, Lars," she said dryly. "Now you know a mess when you see it, maybe you'll learn to keep your bedroom from becoming one."

"What are you doing?"

"Well, this is a combination fall housecleaning and treasure hunt. We've *got* to find that will—and fast."

"But we've already searched the whole house."

"I know." Her forehead wrinkled with worry. "There's something else funny, Lars. I can't find that cup and ball I returned to Aunt Cass when we moved here. She must have hidden it in that drat-ted hidey-hole along with her valuable papers."

"Valuable papers!" I suddenly remembered something Geordie had said. "Spices and gun-powder and valuable papers! That's it!" I exclaimed. Hurrying over to the fireplace, I ran my fingers over the woodwork above the mantel. "Got to be here somewhere," I said, tapping the carving hopefully. "There's a secret door. Come on, Mom, help me find the spring to open it!"

My mother walked over with discouraging calmness. "If you mean the spice closet, I've already checked," she said matter-of-factly.

"H-how did you know about that?" I said.

"I found out a few of Penncroft's secrets—even without George's help," she answered with a grin. It soon faded. "Look, honey, why don't you search the barn? It's an unlikely hiding place, but who knows—maybe that's where the will is."

I quickly downed my after-school snack and rushed out to the barn. Maybe I'd be lucky enough to find Geordie hanging out there again. But when I went inside the great doors and pulled the light cord, there was nothing but the array of folded boxes and a musty smell. Crestfallen, I leaned against the weathered wood of the barn wall and ran my finger lightly over the peg where the riddle had hung.

"That Geordie—he's a riddle, too," I said under my breath. "Why didn't he tell me some magic word I could use to call him when I want him, like 'Open sesame' or 'Bibbedy, bobbedy, boo' or something?"

"'Bibbedy, bobbedy, *boo*'!?" protested an incredulous voice in my ear. "You must be jesting, Lars. No self-respecting shade would respond to such tomfoolery."

I sprang away from the wall. "Geordie! You're back! Now you can tell me what..."

With a chuckle, Geordie reached up and swept the tricorne off his head, swooping it in front as he gave a deep bow. "At your service, sir. What would it please you to know?"

"Everything. But mostly, did Will recover from his wound?"

10

Greene Country Towne/
Whitemarsh

If Father suspected anything, he showed no sign of it as September gave way to October. Although one day he did notice that there were candles missing from the tin box by the fireplace and asked what had happened to them.

Mother and I exchanged startled looks. She was a stickler about truth telling, and I could read her thoughts as if she had spoken them. The candles had gone to light up Grampa's Folly. How could we protect Will without lying to Father? We didn't have to.

"Must've been the mice again, eh, slugabed?" Father said.

"Ah," I yawned, not quite agreeing, though he thought I did. My drowsiness when he'd try to rouse me each morning hadn't escaped Father's notice. He never knew that I'd spent most of each night with

Will. Mother would slip out to the barn when Father and I went off to the orchard lugging the apple barrow.

In late October there was news of another major battle between Washington's forces and the British, this time at Germantown. That night, I told Will how terribly close the Americans had come to victory at Germantown, only to lose once more.

I blathered on, little thinking of the effect on Will, who, though still weak, was nearly healed. It was beginning to appear that his leg would never return to normal, for it could bear little weight. Will was busily whittling a cane to help himself walk.

Several weeks later, I was hauling baskets of apples and pears into the barn, when I saw Will standing at the door of Grampa's Folly.

"Geordie," he said, "I must tell you of my decision."

Relief flooded over me. The strain of secrecy had taken a toll. "That we can tell Father you're here? That you're not going back?"

Will shook his head sadly. "Don't tell Father. Let him think me still with Washington. It'll be true enough tomorrow."

"But, Will, your leg! You can't march or run or . . . or anything." I faltered, remembering the soldiers fleeing and falling near Brandywine.

Will gave his cane a rueful glance. "Aye, but I can still do things to help. Where there's a Will..."

"...there's a way," I finished for him. "So we always say. But surely there are others to do what's necessary, and you—you've already been badly hurt by this war. Why should you go back?" Emotion made my voice crack.

"'Tis said the sevens in 1777 look like gallows for Washington and the other patriot leaders," Will said grimly. "I'll not sit back and watch them hang—not this or any year!"

I stood mute, wanting to beg him not to go. But my silent entreaties, and my mother's spoken ones, fell on ears deafened by determination.

The next day, Father told me to pick up a load of empty kegs and then walked off toward the orchard. This was the chance Will was waiting for. Bidding Mother farewell, he climbed up beside me on the wagon and we started off. All too soon, we came to the fork where our paths divided: me for the cooper's, him for the Continental encampment at Whitemarsh, a few miles north of occupied Philadelphia.

Will gingerly eased himself down to the ground. Then he pulled the cockade off his hat and held it out to me. "I shan't need this now—no more marching into battle for me. Keep it to remember me, Geordie. Farewell."

Will's image blurred through my tear-filled eyes as he limped up the road, leaning stiffly on his cane. I put the cockade inside my tricorne where Father wouldn't see it. Then, setting the hat on my head at a jaunty angle that ill matched the sadness I felt inside, I whipped up my team.

Several days later, I met our gossipy neighbor, Mistress Derry, whose farm bordered our own. I'd always liked her, although her fluttery ways—and her patriot views—drove my father to distraction.

She positively squeaked with excitement. "Ah, Geordie, have you heard the brave news?" she cried.

"News, ma'am?"

"Of the great American victory at Saratoga in New York, don't you know, where I have a cousin— a third cousin, actually, whom I visited as child. What a hoyden she was, to be sure!"

"But the victory, ma'am?" I reminded her.

"Oh my, yes—of course! Whatever was I thinking of? That British general Burgoyne—the dandy they call 'Gentleman Johnny'?" Her bright eyes peered at me eagerly from under the edge of her white mob-cap. "Well, my dear, he has surrendered his entire command—nearly six thousand strong—to our General Gates. Though they do say Benedict Arnold fought like a very dragon and should share the credit. La, these men!" Then Mistress Derry performed one of those conversational leaps that baffled her listeners. "And as for the British soldiers in Philadelphia, why, their behavior is simply abominable! You'd scarcely credit the barbarity!" she spluttered. "Not only have they burned down any number of lovely houses near their picket lines, but they dump all manner of filth in the streets to show how much they hold America in contempt!"

I agreed 'twas shocking in the extreme, and hurriedly bade her good day. As I drove away, I tried to sort out the jumble of elation and frustration I felt at the news of a Continental victory. Why couldn't we have heard about Saratoga before Will left? Maybe then he wouldn't have felt compelled to go.

But gone Will was, and worry over his whereabouts made November lag by, despite the work that filled our days. Father and I toiled from dawn to dusk, driving the team to pull the cider mill wheel round and round its trough to crush the fruit into pomace. Then we'd rake the pomace onto straw mats and carefully press out the juice into the waiting kegs.

One morning early in December when we sat at breakfast, Father lifted his eyes from his porridge and looked at me strangely. There was something about his stern countenance that made me fancy he had found out about Will. I exchanged an uneasy look with my mother as she ladled porridge from the copper kettle into my wooden trencher. At length, Father spoke my name.

"Sir?" I answered.

"Today I want you to take a load of fruit and cider into Philadelphia, to the City Tavern."

"The City Tavern?" my mother said, a puzzled expression on her face. "But I thought they were too elegant to serve country brews. Why, they always have the finest wines from Europe—or so Mistress Derry tells me," she added hastily when Father looked surprised at her unexpected worldly knowledge.

"What with the rebels lobbing cannonballs from Fort Mifflin and putting barricades across the channel, no British ships have been able to bring supplies up the Delaware River to the city, all fall. And even though Fort Mifflin fell a fortnight ago, the taverns in the city must lack sufficient drink. They'll be happy enough to buy from us." Father scraped his trencher clean.

"But, Laban, Geordie is only a boy, and there might be American patrols, stopping countrymen from selling supplies to the British," Mother protested.

"Geordie's been to market in Philadelphia many times. He can avoid the main road and Washington's patrols. He'll come to no harm," Father said.

Mother sank down onto the bench beside me and brushed her hands wearily over her eyes. "And what about our other son? Will he also come to no harm?" she murmured.

Father's face hardened. "Geordie is my only son, Patience."

"I see," my mother whispered. "Thee will disown thy child. I pray thee does not regret it, Laban." She marched out of the room stiffly.

By the set of Father's jaw, I judged it prudent to be on my way without further discussion. Indeed, I was lighthearted at doing so, curious to glimpse life in Philadelphia under British occupation.

'Twas midafternoon when I reached the northern limits of the city, where I quickly saw that totty-headed Mistress Derry had gotten her facts straight. Near the British defenses, blackened wrecks stood where tidy houses once were, and other buildings, though unburned, had gaping holes that gave them *the piteous look of blinded men. My lightheartedness gave way to dull anger over this wanton destruction. I could not bring myself to return the friendly banter of the pickets, who, after sampling a cupful of my perry, waved me through the lines with great cordiality.*

Houses in the main part of the city hadn't been burned. Still, as I drove through the streets I was stunned by the changes enemy occupation had wrought in the once-proud town—second in size only to London in the whole of the British Empire. The first thing I noticed was the absence of white fences around the houses. On my earliest journey into Philadelphia, so young that I still wore a padded "pudding cap" to protect my head as I toddled about, I'd thought the fences were toothy smiles. It was a standing family joke that I'd lisped, "The city is smiling at me!"

The city was smiling no longer. The stench of decay hung over the town like a fog. Every alley was full of makeshift huts and littered with filth, and an open pit full of dead horses added to the putrid smell. Old William Penn, who'd founded Philadelphia almost a century before, would have cried to see the sorry state of his "Greene Country Towne."

But it wasn't only the despoiling of the city that

made me gawk like a country bumpkin. Nay, 'twas seeing what had not changed. For, despite the occupying army, there was much the same hustle and bustle, with people going about their business as usual. Plump matrons still gossiped on doorsteps, leather-aproned apprentices rushed about on errands, gentlemen strolled past shop windows laden with silks and satins, and fashionable young ladies flirted with admirers on street corners—admirers clad in scarlet uniforms.

"The only things outnumbering redcoats are blackflies," I muttered to myself as I came to the Pennsylvania State House. I peered up at the soaring tower to see the great bell that had been rung to summon folk to hear the Declaration of Independence.

The tower was empty. Mystified, my eyes fell to the second-story windows that fronted the Long Gallery—site of elegant state dinners. But Congress had long since fled the city, and no elegant diners peered down from the Long Gallery today. Instead, I spied a crowd of gaunt, ragged men, eyes huge in their skeletal faces.

Horrified, I reined in Daisy and Buttercup. Women in sober Quaker clothes were carrying baskets toward the State House door.

I called out to one. "Mistress, who are those men in the Long Gallery?"

"The British are using it as a prison," she answered sadly, "for wounded Continental soldiers captured at Brandywine and Germantown. The blockade made food scarce in the city, and the British expect the Americans to supply food for their own men held here. The American army can barely feed itself, let alone spare any for these poor starved creatures."

I bade her wait. "Here—take some apples for the prisoners," I called to her, trying not to think how my father would thrash me should he learn what I had done. "And a barrel of perry as well."

"Bless you, lad," she said softly.

Embarrassed, I pointed up at the empty bell tower and asked, "Where is the great bell . . . and . . . and where are all the fences?"

"The bell was moved to Allentown so the British couldn't melt it down for bullets. And the fences have gone for firewood. But not for those poor men imprisoned yonder. 'Tis most bitterly cold inside, and they have no fire at all."

Wishing I'd brought in a wagonload of firewood, I jumped down, unloaded a keg and basket and carried them to the State House door. Then I climbed back on the wagon, shivering as I thought of the men upstairs.

The situation was quite different at the elegant City Tavern, where a great blazing fire warmed the *patrons to a nicety. Threading my way through the crowd of periwigged merchants and elegant officers to the Bar Room, I soon found the manager, Daniel Smith. Much to my relief, he jumped at my shy offer of fruit and drink.*

"Of course, lad, I'll take everything you've got—and whatever else you can bring me. Our supplies are in a sorry state, and the British officers are like to drink my cellar dry. Here, I'll get someone to help you unload. Billy?"

At his summons, a man poked his head out from the hallway door—a man dressed in servant's livery, who leaned on a hand-whittled cane and looked at me with eyes full of warning.

'Twas Will. As if in a dream, I followed him outside. "Will, what in blazes are you . . ."

Will looked about furtively. "Shhh. Billy, if you please," he whispered out of the side of his mouth in a way that, under ordinary circumstances, would have made me laugh. "And don't stand about like a ninnyhammer! Help me with these barrels."

"But Wi—er, Billy, how do you come to be here?"

"Just as I thought, I proved unfit to be a foot soldier, so I've come into the city as a sort of a spy."

"A spy? Wi—Billy? You're a spy for Washington?" My heart thumped in sudden fear.

Will clapped his hand over my mouth. "You needn't proclaim it from the rooftops, else I'll be on one of those gallows we talked of earlier." He took his hand away. "It's not so bad, Geordie," he said with a smile. "At least I have a snug pallet to sleep on up in the attic, and Little Smith allows me to dine on table scraps. It may be only broken meats, but that's still better than camp fare. Come on, let's get these inside."

He lifted a barrel to his shoulder. Then, balancing on his cane, he turned toward the tavern. There was certainly nothing wrong with his arms, I marveled, struggling under the weight of my own load. We carried the barrels into the cellar storeroom where we could talk out of earshot of any passersby.

I felt as if I might burst with questions. "B-but what are you doing at the City Tavern?" was my first.

"I work here for Little Smith and listen to the idle chatter amongst the British officers. You'd be agog to know how much they reveal about military plans whilst in their cups."

"But how do you get word back to Washington?"

"Up until now a man and boy have carried messages for me, but the man has fallen under suspicion and rejoined Washington. That leaves only the boy, and..." He hesitated, then looked at me speculatively. "Geordie, I must ask for your help. I've some

155

important information—a British orderly book. It details General Howe's plans to attack the American encampment at Whitemarsh. Could you help the boy get it through to Washington? If the camp is taken by surprise, it would be the end for us, outnumbered as we are."

For a brief moment, the three gallows in 1777 seemed to loom before my eyes so that I could see the very nooses swaying in the icy December wind. With an effort, I said, "Aye, Will, just tell me what to do."

"Good lad." He touched my shoulder. "The boy, Sandy, will guide you up to Whitemarsh. He'll be waiting for you at dusk past the British lines. As you don't know each other by sight, you'll have to use the password."

"Which is?"

Will grinned. "Well, most times we use the saying, 'Where there's a Will, there's a way.' In fact, Sandy has my signet ring with that Latin inscription. It's been an invaluable way to identify him to other couriers."

"'Ubi voluntas via ibi est,'" I murmured.

Will grinned and shrugged his shoulders, looking a little sheepish. "That's all I could think of, but it's worked well so far. Now, since it may be too dark to see the ring, you'll have to use the other signal. Whistle 'The Riddle Song.'"

"All the way to Whitemarsh?"

"Nay, you dolt. Only for a mile or two past the British lines. Sandy will be lurking about somewhere close by and hear you. He's a clever lad and will rise to the occasion, I warrant."

"You warrant my neck, Will," I said soberly.

"They'll not hang you for a spy. Only an official agent out of uniform behind enemy lines would meet such an end."

Like you, I thought, my brow pinpricked by cold sweat.

"Mind, give it into no other hands than those of Washington himself. The American army is riddled with Tory spies—almost as riddled as the city is with ours," Will added with a wink.

We quickly fetched the orderly book from his attic room, then went down to the wagon, where I stood sentry whilst he wedged the book into a crack of the wagon seat. Then, bidding him a tense farewell, I drove off toward the British defenses.

Luckily the same pickets were on duty, and their fond memories of my perry cleared my way through the lines. Still, once outside the city, I grew more pudding-hearted with each turn of the wheels. It was with great difficulty that I puckered my dry lips and whistled "The Riddle Song." I was so beset with nerves that I failed to see the slight figure emerge from the trees next to the road until I was virtually upon him. Fearing I'd run him down, I pulled the team to a halt and jumped down to investigate— only to fall flat on my breeches' bottom. A distinct chuckle greeted the spectacle I presented.

I leaped to my feet to confront this person who dared to enjoy my fall. Peering back at me was a boy so slight that the top of his head came only to my shoulder. Before I could say anything, he spoke urgently in a low voice.

"Where there's a Will, I presume there's a way?" He held out his palm. Will's signet ring lay upon it.

I stood agape. This infant was to be my partner? Watching him stick the ring into his breeches pocket, I wondered why he didn't wear it, then realized that it was probably much too large for his boy-size hands. Will himself hadn't grown into it until he reached sixteen or so.

"There's no time to tarry. Help me up and let's be on our way," said the lad imperiously, clapping on a tricorne so that it perched crookedly on his sand-colored hair.

"H-help you up?" I asked.

He laughed. "Are you a half-wit as well as a clumsy?"

I thrust my fist under his nose. "When we have time enough, I'll show you who's a clumsy half-wit," I hissed.

The boy merely put his hand on top of my fist, turned neatly and vaulted into the wagon seat. "Hurry up, boy, there are thieves about, pretending to be patriot patrols. They'll take your wagon if they catch us."

I needed no further urging. In an instant I was beside the impudent boy, and we were headed north on Germantown Pike. We spoke but little on our way, and I kept the horses to a walk in the gathering darkness, with Sandy barking out which turn to take every time we reached a crossroad.

My courage was badly frayed by the time we reached the American pickets, but my companion was undaunted by their challenge. Calmly stating that we carried important information from Philadelphia, he requested an escort to General Washington. We were led through the encampment, and I saw that these soldiers were in some ways worse off than those imprisoned in the State House. Most were bedding down on frozen ruts on the ground, and the food I saw cooking over the campfires was none too plentiful.

I had little time to ponder their plight, however, for soon we entered the house where General Washington was headquartered. This time the general was wigless and wearing a damask dressing gown. Even seated at a desk he seemed to tower over us, and his eyes were as penetrating as when they had first beheld Squire Cheyney and me at Brandywine.

"What is it?" he said in a voice full of weariness.

Sandy stood at attention. "Here, your Excellency. A British orderly book with battle orders for an attack here at Whitemarsh." Sandy's self-possession filled me with intense envy.

Washington straightened up. "We had word that there was a move afoot, and this looks to give us the details." He quickly gave the book to an aide, directing him to report on its contents with all dispatch. Then, turning back to me, the general said, "But have I not seen you before, boy?"

"At Brandywine, sir, with Squire Cheyney," I mumbled shyly.

"And you refused to take up the drum. The offer's still open—to both of you." His lips parted in a startling smile, revealing darkened teeth that were patently false. For an instant it seemed as if I were reliving the scene with that nauseating Owens. Once again another boy would get the glory of drumming with the Continentals, and I would have to go home to my parents. Jealousy swept over me, but it evaporated when I saw Sandy shake his head in a decided no. What's more, his face was so crimson he looked as if he were about to cry.

I bowed my head and could feel my own face flushing as I mumbled, "I cannot, your...your Excellency. My father is a king's man and already brokenhearted because my brother has joined you."

Washington's face furrowed with sadness. "This terrible war that severs families." He paused, then added, "Then I thank you doubly for your service to Independency. It takes strength to defy both king and father. Would that all my men were as committed. Though battle-hardened, my troops still desert in droves. The officers, too, resign over imagined slights and..." Washington glanced at us as if suddenly remembering our presence. "You may go, now," he said gruffly.

I nodded dumbly and rushed out of the tent. Sandy didn't catch up with me until I reached the wagon.

"Geordie—wait! 'Tis impossible for me to stay here. I must return to the city. I'm afraid...Will you take me back?"

In the moonlight, his face looked pinched with anxiety. I was thunderstruck that this boy, pluck to the backbone, feared to stay in the American camp. His speck of cowardice cheered me, however, and cemented our friendship more than all his spunk.

"Aye, I'll take ye. Pray that my father will be so pleased by the gold coins from the City Tavern that he won't inquire too closely about my late return."

We laughed and set off into the moonlit night in perfect charity with one another—firm friends despite our differences.

Geordie sat lost in thought for a moment. I hated to interrupt his musing, but there were so many things I had to find out. Had Will made it through the British occupation of Philadelphia without being caught as a spy? Or had those gallows in 1777 proved fatal for Geordie's brother?

Before I could ask, my mother came into the barn carrying a plate of cookies. Naturally, this drove Geordie away.

Mom anxiously scanned my face. "Don't worry, honey, we'll find that will. Just keep your spirits up."

"I'll do my best," I promised solemnly.

11

Seeing Sights in Center City

The subway train pulled up at Independence Square in Philadelphia and I was the first to hop off onto the platform. "Come on—I want to beat the tourists. Hurry up!" I urged.

My parents exchanged looks of amazement.

"Are you feeling all right, Lars?" my mother asked. "First you get up early on a Saturday morning without being crowbarred out of bed. And now you're so eager to get there you want us to sprint! Erik, are you sure this is really our son?"

Dad chuckled. "I remember how underwhelmed you were about visiting historical sights, Lars, and now you're begging to go places I've never even heard of."

"Whitemarsh—it's Fort Washington State

Park," I said eagerly. "Can we go up there some-time?"

"I guess so—after I recover from the shock! It wasn't too long ago that nothing would have gotten you to sightsee in Center City. I never saw such a rapid change of spirits in my life!" Dad teased.

Spirits had had more to do with my new attitude than they would ever know, but I could hardly say *that*.

"Look, there's the Liberty Bell! Let's get in line to see it, Erik!" my mother said, giving Dad's arm a gentle pull.

"Aw, it wasn't even here during the British occupation," I protested. "They hauled it up to Allentown so the British wouldn't melt it down for bullets. Let's go to the State House."

"I don't remember any State House here," Mom said, with a puzzled look. "I thought the big attraction was Independence Hall."

"Yeah, I forgot, that was the *old* name," I said, rushing to add a plea that we eat lunch at the City Tavern.

Dad warded off my request. "One thing at a time, Lars!"

"But that's a great idea, Erik," Mom put in.

"They've rebuilt the City Tavern exactly as it was during the Revolution—authentic eighteenth-century food and costumed waiters, the whole bit."

Dad relented. "All right, we'll eat there. But only after we check out Independence Hall *and* the Liberty Bell."

"When I visited here as a little girl, the Liberty Bell was still inside Independence Hall," Mom recalled with a faraway look. "You should have seen how Aunt Cass and George carried on, you'd think it was all a family shrine."

Intrigued by her words, I joined the line and filed past the massive bell. Then I herded my folks across the street to Independence Hall. My eyes flew to the second-story windows, half expecting to see the gaunt faces of American prisoners looking down from the Long Gallery.

With other tourists, we were parceled into groups by park guides to tour the historic rooms. I drank in the guide's every word as eagerly as the prisoners had probably drunk Geordie's perry on that long-ago day.

When we came out of Independence Hall into the bright sunshine, Mom announced it was lunchtime and took out her map to look for the City Tavern.

"Let's stop at the Portrait Gallery," Dad suggested. "It's right on the way. Maybe some Hargreaves ancestors are pictured there. Surely some of 'em must have been around at the time of the Revolution."

Mom grinned. "From what Aunt Cass told me, I don't think my ancestors exactly covered themselves with patriotic glory. Apparently at least one of them was a staunch Tory."

Dad put his hand to his forehead. "Shocking!" he squeaked.

I didn't know Geordie's last name, so there was no way I could find his picture. I asked if we could skip the gallery.

"I guess so. We'll go another day. After all, we'll be living here a good long time," Dad replied.

Mom's face fell. "At least I hope so," she murmured. Then she brightened, her attention caught by a horse-drawn carriage clattering past. "Oh, look! That's something new!" She chuckled. "Or old, actually, but new since my last visit."

Dad said, "Shall we take a carriage ride?"

"I'd love to, but I'd hate to breathe in all the smelly exhaust from the traffic," Mom said, wrinkling up her nose.

I laughed. "At least it doesn't smell as bad as it

did during the British occupation when there were dead horses and . . ."

Dad broke in. "Your teacher has certainly filled you in on all the gory details," he said dryly.

Luckily, right then we arrived at the City Tavern. I looked up at the brick building and wondered which attic window had been Will's. Mom and Dad herded me inside into a long hallway. I could see waitresses in mobcaps and long dresses and waiters in clothes like Geordie's. One costumed waiter came out into the hallway. He carried a wooden keg on his shoulder, a cane in his hand.

Stunned, I shouted out, "Will!"

The young man turned, peered at us, and put down the keg. "Sir, Madam. May I serve you in some way?"

I thought fast. "Will—will—you tell us where to sit?"

"The serving wench will escort you directly. Just go into the Coffee Room yonder." Then, with a bow to my mother, he picked up his burden and limped down the stairs.

Astonishment rooted me to the floor. Did Will haunt the City Tavern? It was, after all, a great place for him to hang out, camouflaged by the colonial outfits of the staff.

Mom was twittering about the Tavern's atmosphere as we sat down. "They really do a great job here, dressing and acting like it's the eighteenth century. I especially loved the bow!"

The costumed waitress handed each of us a large menu that looked as if it were written on parchment.

"Interesting," said Dad, reading his menu. "This was quite a popular spot with the Founding Fathers—John Adams called it 'the most genteel tavern in America'—and they all came here to celebrate after signing the Declaration of Independence. Wonder what drink they used to toast the big event?"

Mom replied, "Some kind of toddy or punch, I imagine."

Her words gave me an idea. When the waitress came to take our order, I told her I wanted the Tavern pasty. Then, gathering my courage, I went on, "And for a drink I think I'll have perry."

Mom laughed and said, "My, what adult tastes you're getting, Lars! I never thought you'd forego soda pop for *that*."

I could hardly wait to see if I'd get what I requested and watched eagle-eyed as the waitress placed a green bottle in front of me. Then I read the label. It said "Perrier."

After lunch, we visited other historic sites that Geordie hadn't mentioned. On the drive home, Dad complimented me on my improved attitude about living in Pennsylvania.

"I know it hasn't been easy for you, and we're both proud of how well you've handled it."

I squirmed a little in the backseat. "But I haven't . . . that is, I mean . . . well, Aunt Cass helped a lot."

Mom beamed at me. "Just the same, we're proud of you."

When we turned off Seek-No-Further Pike and passed the Penncroft Farm sign, I remembered the first time I'd seen it. It was amazing how different I felt now.

"Why, that's Judge Bank's car," Mom exclaimed in a worried tone. "I wonder what he's come all this way for!"

The judge stepped out of his car and came over to us. "Erik, Sandra, L. George," he said solemnly. Then, clearing his throat, he said, "I'm afraid I'm here as your lawyer, not just as your friend. Edward Owens has filed suit in the probate court."

My mother's eyes flashed. "If only we could find that new will! Couldn't we stall by asking the Hargreaveses to vouch for the fact she *did* write a new will? They witnessed it."

"Owens found out about it and cornered Ellen Hargreaves to ask her what she had seen of the will when she signed it. At first Ellen said she hadn't seen anything. You know that witnesses don't usually read the documents they sign; they only verify the signature of the main parties involved. But when Owens asked if she had happened to see his name anywhere on the page, she admitted that she had noticed it was in there because Cass had written the name in especially elaborate letters. The large Roman numeral *IX* caught her eye."

My mother protested, "But *that* doesn't prove anything!"

"Owens thinks it does. And because Cass's old will clearly left the farm to him, he thinks it's enough to win his case. Owens always was a little nutty about memorializing his ancestors, but now I think he's really gone off the deep end. He says you're living here illegally."

Mom stamped her foot. "If only we could find that will! I can't bear to leave Penncroft now!"

Dad put his arm around her. "Surely it will turn

up, Sandra, if we can just figure out where she could have . . . Lars, you've probably poked around in all the nooks and crannies here. Lars?"

But I didn't answer. I ran from the adults as fast as I could into the orchard to be alone with my fears. We might really have to leave Penncroft Farm. And I realized I couldn't bear that any more than Mom could.

I was so upset, I went to bed that night with a throbbing headache. The next morning, I woke up with a sore throat and a red rash all over my body. Even though every swallow was agony, it was actually more pleasant than going to school and facing Eddie Owens.

Mom took me in for a throat culture, and the next day the doctor called to say that I definitely had a strep infection. Mom told me that the rash along with strep throat meant I had scarlet fever.

My throat was so sore I could only croak, "Scarlet fever! I thought that was extinct!"

"It's still around, but penicillin will take care of it. I'm going into town to pick up your prescription. Try and get some rest, honey. When I get back I'll make you chicken soup or whatever else you think you can swallow. Sleep tight!"

I could hear her footsteps going down the stairs

and out the back door. Soon the sound of her car heading down the road faded away, and I drifted off into a fevered sleep. After what seemed only an instant, my eyes fluttered open.

There, sprawled across the window seat, was Geordie. The buckles on his shoes caught the light from the window like signal mirrors. When Geordie saw I was awake, he came over to the bed. "Good morrow, Lars. You appear to be a mite doleful."

"My throat is really sore."

"I hope it doesn't turn putrid."

The word made my stomach lurch. "Putrid!" I said feebly.

Geordie leaned over me. "Putrid throat was what nearly carried off Will."

I tried to sit up, then fell back against my pillows, swallowing painfully. "I thought he was wounded in the *leg*!"

"Aye, but 'twas putrid throat laid him low at Valley Forge. Sandy and I truly feared for his life."

"You saw Sandy again?"

Geordie smiled to himself. "I saw Sandy more than you'd think. But I'd best commence my story properly and tell you the whole. At the very least it may divert your mind from your own miseries."

12

Not Worth
a Continental

After I returned from Whitemarsh, life at Penncroft
Farm went on much as usual. Day after day, I helped
Father with the winter pruning, trimming branches
to allow more room for fruit to grow and enable us to
reach it from atop our ladders. Night after night, we
sat by the fire—I shaking wheat through the riddle,
Father repairing baskets, Mother spinning or knitting.
Our hands were busy, but our tongues were silenced
by our secrets, all discourse banished by discord.

I didn't tell Mother that Will was no longer a regular solider, though doing so might have eased her
Quaker conscience. Knowing her son risked the gallows to spy in enemy-held Philadelphia would surely
not have eased her heart.

For several weeks, I was in a fever to hear if

General Howe had indeed attacked the American encampment and what the outcome had been. The mails and newspapers were sorely disrupted by the occupation of the capital, however, and I could hardly ask Father for such news without betraying my interest—not to mention my growing attachment to what he still called the rebel cause. Thus I was mightily pleased when I happened upon Squire Cheyney.

The squire seemed right glad to see me. "Hullo, young Geordie," he bellowed like a large, friendly bull. "How's your mule of a father? Does he know of your bravery at Chadd's Ford?"

I twisted my hat in my hands and replied bashfully, "Nay."

"At least we Americans showed our mettle, though we were outmaneuvered. And at Germantown we came closer to victory..."

"Squire," I broke in, too eager for news to be properly polite to my elders. "What happened at Whitemarsh?"

His laughter boomed out. "Whitemarsh? Why, General Sir Billy Howe marched his army up to attack, and there was Washington on a high hill ready and waiting for him. Howe tried to lure Washington down for a fight, but His Excellency wouldn't be drawn. He stayed up in those fortresslike hills, and Howe's cannonballs bounced off the very trees without hurting anybody. Sir Billy fumed and fretted for a day or two, then marched his troops back to Philadelphia. Puts me in mind of the song: 'The king of France, with forty thousand men, marched up the hill and then marched down again.' Ah, I would have paid real gold for the chance to see those redcoats crawling back to Philadelphia."

"Is Washington still at Whitemarsh, then?" I asked.

"Nay, lad, they're decamped. Gone into winter quarters at Valley Forge. 'Tain't gentlemanly for armies to fight in the wintertime, it seems. So the Continentals are living like beggars at Valley Forge, while the British carouse like gentlemen in Philadelphia," he said, grimacing.

"Valley Forge? But how can ten thousand men find shelter there?" I looked about me at the snowdrifts and remembered the soldiers shivering at Whitemarsh.

The squire snorted. "The merchants of Philadelphia insisted that the army stay nearby or they'd cut off all their support. Besides, it's my guess that Washington wants to stay between Howe's army and the

American supplies stored at Reading—especially since the redcoats burned the materiel stored at Valley Forge when they raided it after Brandywine."

For the first time, I was glad Will was a spy in Philadelphia. Dangerous as that was, at least he slept in a warm garret and had table scraps to eat.

I took my leave of the squire and started for home. As I guided the reluctant team down the snow-laden pike, I found myself unconsciously humming "The King of France." Then, as the wind pierced my old brown woolen cloak, I tried to warm myself by thinking about the hot stew, fresh-baked bread, and mulled cider my mother had promised to have ready.

It was to be a special treat in these lean times. Most of our customers had paid us in Continentals— the paper money issued by the Continental Congress. These bills were worth so little that folks had taken to disparaging the value of something by saying it was "not worth a Continental" (an expression Father applied as freely to American soldiery as he did to American currency). In any case, we sorely missed the English pounds that we would have gained had the war—and Congress—not cut off British trade. Indeed, we had been forced to barter for necessities with food we ordinarily kept for our own use through the long winter. As a result, our family larder was ill-stocked.

Thus, my mouth was watering when I clattered into the kitchen, stomping my snowy boots at the door. But no heady aromas greeted me; no steaming mugs waited on the hob. No clack issued from Mother's loom, nor was there even the gentlest of squeaks from her spinning wheel. The fireplace held only stone-cold ashes, and the room was filled with a strange, bewildering silence.

Apprehension swept over me, bringing a chill colder than the January wind outside. I had never known my mother to allow the fire to die upon our hearth. Even when we were gone from the house, we always banked the embers with great care to rekindle upon our return.

I pulled off my dripping boots and ran stocking-footed up the dark, narrow stairs. As I reached the door to my parents' bedchamber, it opened and my mother appeared, her face as pale as death. She came into the corridor and shut the door behind her.

"'Tis thy father, Geordie. He was pruning one of the old peach trees by the stone wall. He fell and struck his head . . . and cannot speak. Or . . . or move," she said softly, bowing her head.

I went over to her. "How . . . how did you get him back here?"

"Mistress Derry happened by in her sledge, and we managed to get him into it with the loading pulley. Then her husband helped . . ."

I dashed away some tears. A lump came into my throat, making it difficult to speak. "Can I see him?" I whispered.

"Not just now. The doctor is in leeching him."

I shuddered at the thought of those repulsive leeches being deliberately fastened to my father's skin to suck out the bad blood.

"I'll go rekindle the fire," I said numbly. As if in a nightmare, I trudged blindly back downstairs.

The nightmare stretched on for more than a month. My mother spent every waking moment at my father's side, but he gave no sign that he was aware of her daytime presence, or of mine at night. The weeks went by in slow, weary procession.

One February afternoon I was in the barn quartering apples to make into apple butter. I stuck apple after apple into the hole in the bench and thrust down the sectioned plunger. The cut apples fell out into the basket below. Somehow the rhythm of the task and my own lack of sleep smoothed the rough edges from my cares, and I nearly fell asleep at my work. That was probably why it took me a moment to realize someone was saying, "Where there's a Will, there's a way."

Poking through the barn door was Sandy's towhead, his tricorne askew as usual. He looked much the same except for his reddened nose and his billowy blue cape.

I exclaimed, "Sandy? How do you come to be here?"

"On foot!" He sat down in the straw.

"Nay, you doodle! I mean *why* did you come? And did you hear about Whitemarsh? D'you reckon the orderly book did the trick?"

"Surely helped." Sandy grinned, then his face turned solemn.

My elation vanished. Sudden fear made me feel burning hot and icy cold at the same time. "It isn't Will, is it?" I whispered.

"Aye. He's sick, Geordie. Up at Valley Forge. He had to flee the city because Little Smith discovered what he was up to; directly after he arrived at camp, your brother came down with putrid fever. He's in the hospital for Wayne's brigade—a flying hospital, they call it, though I cannot fathom why. 'Tis only a damp and crowded hut. Doctors there can do little but leech and pray. I've been nursing Billy when I can, but I'm often called away from camp. He needs constant attendance and nourishing food. They all do," he added emotionally. Pausing to collect himself, he glanced at me and went on. "I thought perhaps your mother..."

I shook my head sadly. "My father is gravely injured, Sandy. I doubt my mother can leave him, even for Will."

"Then you must come, Geordie. Else he'll die."

I looked at Sandy, thinking of all the farmwork to be done and my mother's tired face. Then I pictured Will lying sick and fevered at Valley Forge and knew what I must do. "Come on, let's tell my mother."

Sandy shrank back. "Nay, you go. I'll wait here for you."

I'd never met anyone who was such a mixture of bravado and bashfulness, but I had little time to think upon such oddities. I flew up the stairs to the sick chamber. My mother received the news about Will calmly. "Yes, of course thee must go. Master Derry will help me with the chores," she said softly. "Ride one of the horses. Would that I could go in thy place, but..." She looked down at Father's face, his eyes shut, his ears unhearing, and sighed. "The doctor says Laban is a mite better. Perhaps when thee return he'll be himself again." With a weak smile, she urged me to take the copper kettle and fill it with food. "And, Geordie, put in some apples to make Will some hot applesauce. He ate it by the bucketful when he was a lad." Her gray eyes filled with tears as I turned away.

I made haste to fill the copper kettle with apples and other food from the scant stores in the cellar. An impulse sent me up to the attic. I stood for a second, staring down at our side-by-side beds, remembering how Will had loved to apple-pie my sheets. I snatched up his old comforter and raced back to the barn. There I quickly bridled Buttercup.

"Come on, then," I said, motioning Sandy to climb onto Buttercup's bare swayed back.

Sandy paused a moment, looking oddly uncertain. Then, taking a deep breath, he threw his leg over. I climbed on behind and we started off at a slow plod for Valley Forge.

It was nearly dark when we forded Valley Creek and entered the American camp. The valley was dotted with fires, but the figures crouched around them seemed scarcely human. Most of the men clutched ragged pieces of blanket about them, and few wore real pants. At first I thought it impressive that so many wore matching white gaiters from the knee to the foot. But a brief flare from one of the fires revealed that what I saw was a white, frigid flesh—nearly as white as the snow on the ground under the men's bare feet.

Suddenly a strange moaning chant began, growing louder as it spread from campfire to campfire. "No meat, no meat, no meat, no meat," swelled the sound as it rolled eerily through the valley. Then the words changed, and the growling chorus rose in pitch and speed. "No meat, no bread, no food, no clothes, no broth, no ale, no soldier!"

Sandy shook his head gravely. "What do you expect? They're cold and hungry—they've had no real rations for nearly a week. They go on like this for hours sometimes. Strange, but just chanting seems to help them endure it."

I looked at the soldiers huddled over the smoking campfires and wondered what made them stay in the face of such profound misery. If only my father could see what these men endured—surely even he would see the worth of these Continentals.

I sighed and asked Sandy where my brother was.

"Back of Wayne's brigade near the outer defenses. Not far," he said. We plodded up a hill and found the flying hospital—a large hut among smaller huts. We slid off Buttercup and looped her reins around a nearby stump. With a sinking heart, I followed Sandy's slight figure to the hospital door.

It was monstrous gloomy inside. On the wall burned one small rushlight, flickering and smoking badly. The smoke was almost welcome, however: It helped to mask the otherwise unbearable stench. Rough-hewn beds, stacked three high, reached nearly to the log rafters. On each bed, and on the floor, men were packed together on straw filthier than my father would have allowed in our pigsty.

"Over here," whispered Sandy, moving toward the bottom of a triple bunk. "He's alone, you see. Putrid fever victims have that luxury. Usually they're sent to hospitals outside the camp, but those are too crowded to take him."

Will lay on his straw, his bare legs sticking out below the small remnant of blanket he clutched to his chest.

I reached out and felt his face. It was burning hot. "Will. It's Geordie. I've come to take care of you," I murmured.

"Geordie?" he said, his voice hoarse beyond all recognition. "You shouldn't have come. You'll take the infection. Go . . . go away." He struggled to sit up, and moaned with pain.

I gently pushed him back down against the straw. "Don't you worry about anything except getting well. I am come to help you, Will. Mother sent food. And here's the cover from your bedstead at home. Remember?" I spread it over him. He only moaned again and drifted off to sleep.

Sandy touched my arm and beckoned me to the hut door, where the February wind whistled through the cracks. "I must leave," he said, "but I'll send someone to help you get settled. You'd best sleep alongside Buttercup. So many horses have starved for lack of forage that there are not enough to pull the artillery should the British attack, so private horses are liable to be confiscated. You must stay close to her until it's known you're only visiting to nurse your brother. Besides," Sandy added with a lopsided grin, "when a man is hungry enough, even a horse might seem a great delicacy."

"You don't mean these men have been eating their horses!" I said, genuinely shocked.

"No—at least, not that I've seen. But they've been without meat for a long time now. So you'd best bundle with Buttercup—at least she'll keep you warm!"

"But where are you . . ."

Sandy's eyes fell. "Oh, I hang around here and

there. But now you've arrived, I'll be easier about leaving Billy. He's like a brother to me, and I couldn't bear it if he should . . ." He manfully choked back a sob and straightened his shoulders. With an odd, desperate glance at me, he went out into the darkness.

Will's haggard appearance made me feel like sobbing myself. Then I thought to make him something hot and soothing to eat when he awoke. I busied myself cutting up some of the apples I'd brought. I put them into the copper kettle and went outside. I scooped up some snow and added it to the apples, then set the kettle over the coals. I felt bad doing this in front of the hungry soldiers ringing the campfire, but after I explained it was for my sick brother, they gamely wished me luck in nursing him. Still, they watched the simmering applesauce with longing eyes. To take their minds off their empty stomachs, once again they took up their gloomy refrain: "No meat, no food, no shoes, no breeches, no soldier!"

When the applesauce was done, I started into the hut with the kettle. Just then, a shadowy form appeared behind me.

"Geordie?"

"Aye?" I was so startled, I nearly dropped the kettle.

"I've been ordered to show you about."

This time it was my jaw that nearly dropped to the floor. It was Ned Owens, still as pudgy as ever, though now dressed in the full regalia of a drummer boy. His nose wrinkled in disdain at the smell of sickness and smoke permeating the hospital hut.

His disdain gave me back my tongue. "Ned Owens. How is it you look so stout in the midst of this near starvation?"

"Let's just say I know which side my bread is buttered on."

"Obviously," I muttered scornfully.

"And I know the important people in this camp."

"You mean Washington?"

"Nay, I mean Inspector General Conway." His voice dropped to a conspiratorial whisper. "He says Congress will soon replace Washington with Gates as commander in chief. And as Conway is a favorite with Gates and I am a favorite with Conway..." Under my astonished gaze Owens preened himself, smoothing down his blue tunic and fingering the brass buttons. "Inspector General Conway has made me his aide, so I sleep at his headquarters, whilst that Sandy bunks down at Washington's headquarters, no less." He sniffed disdainfully. "Lady Washington mollycoddles that smock-faced toad-eater Sandy something shameful. But they'll all be sorry when Gates

and Conway take over," he added in a venomous voice.

"We'll all be sorry if that craven coward Conway takes over anything," someone hissed from atop one of the bunks.

Owens laughed aloud. But it was a sound full of scorn, not mirth. "I don't know how Sandy expected me to help you. I seldom come to this part of the camp."

Through clenched teeth I said, "I won't trouble you further then, Owens. I'm sure I can learn what is necessary from these good fellows."

Even in the uncertain candlelight, I could see Ned's outrage at my rejection of his reluctant offer of aid. Quickly collecting himself, however, he sketched an insolent bow and left. No sooner had the door swung shut on its leathern hinges than gruff voices sounded in the flickering shadows.

"That Owens brat is as much of a disgrace as his father, who turns a handsome profit selling the army weevily food and shoddy uniforms."

"Aye, the elder Owens was as fervent a Tory as the king himself until he realized that Independency might erase his debt to his London suppliers. Then didn't he turn every inch the patriot! But he won't accept anything but gold coin in payment—no worthless

Continental paper money for him. Save that to pay the soldiers!"

"As for Conway," the speaker audibly spat, "he's a coward and a braggart who's gulled the Congress into making him inspector general. He's bent on stirring up trouble for General Washington—with no thought for anything but his own glory."

"I fancy both Conway and Owens would be much improved by a new coat in the very latest fashion: tar and feathers," another said with an exaggerated simper.

"As for me," the first speaker went on, "I say that Washington is the only one we follow. No Washington, no army!"

"No Washington, no army!" a voice outside took up the chant, and it spread around the camp in the same manner as the other, earlier, more ominous cry. "No Washington, no army!" rasped hundreds, thousands of voices, until the wintry hills echoed with the brave words.

The noise woke Will up. I managed to get a little of the applesauce into him, then parceled out what remained to the other sick men in the hut. Afterward, drooping with fatigue, I went out to fall asleep huddled next to Buttercup—surely the unlikeliest tempting morsel in history.

13

Tempered at
the Forge

I don't know if it was the doctor's leeches or my applesauce that brought my brother through that terrible sickness, but after I'd been at Valley Forge for about a fortnight, Will's fever broke. One morning he awoke acting a little like his old, teasing self, though still exceedingly weak.

As I attempted to bathe away some of the scabies and lice on his skin and hair, he looked down ruefully at the scarlet rash on his chest. "Just look at this, Geordie," he said. "I'm as red as a lobsterback—and that without a tunic on!"

One of the other men guffawed. "You'll soon be reduced to the official colors—Continental buff and blue—like most of us. We're nearly stripped to the buff and blue with cold!" By then I'd learned that making such pitiful jokes was one of the only weapons these poor fellows had in facing their foes: hunger, cold, and grinding boredom. Not that anyone was actually starving to death—from time to time supplies did arrive at camp, but the roads were often nearly impassable. And sometimes the wagoners lightened loads by draining off the saltwater that preserved the food, so that what did arrive was rotten. When that happened, the soldiers survived on firecake, a tasteless mixture of flour and water charred over the fire. They even joked about this, saying they varied their diet by sometimes eating "firecakes and water" and other times eating "water and firecakes."

Oddly enough, the British seemed to be the least of the soldiers' worries. Rumor said that General Howe couldn't bear to leave the comfort of his Philadelphia mansion—or the company of a certain Tory lady—to attack the weakened American forces at Valley Forge. The men made many a mock toast with cups of melted, dirty snow to the health of the lady in question.

Sandy never joined in these rowdy measures. Owens had been right about my friend having a snug billet in Washington's headquarters—Isaac Potts's stone house near the Y made by the Schuylkill River and Valley Creek. Passing Washington's quarters one day, I peered curiously through the window. There sat

Sandy, holding up a figure eight of yarn between his hands whilst a lace-capped Lady Washington rewound the wool into a snug ball.

When I next saw Sandy, I teased him about playing lapdog to Lady Washington. He refused to speak of it. He did tell me, however, each time he was to leave camp. After our experience at Whitemarsh together, I presumed he was going into Philadelphia for messages from American agents.

Whenever he returned to Valley Forge, he would help me take care of my brother. When Will slept, Sandy and I would explore the camp. My friend delighted in the irony of many of the place-names of Valley Forge, such as Fatlands Ford and Mount Joy.

The Grand Parade was another name we thought grimly amusing. Upon that barren expanse the men with strength enough tried to drill, but with little enthusiasm and less skill. The officers scarcely knew more than the men, and no two officers used the same commands. It was not much of a parade, and only a zany would have dubbed it grand.

One afternoon on the Grand Parade, we watched as drummers and fifers straggled out to form two crooked lines. Between the lines marched two officers, one with his uniform coat inside out and backward. The other drew the sword from the scabbard of the oddly dressed officer, raised it high, and broke it over his own knee. Immediately, two private soldiers led out a scrawny-looking horse and placed the offending officer backward on its bare back. As the fifers and drummers struck up a march, the two soldiers swatted the animal's bony rump until it headed out of camp. A few jeers and hisses arose, but most soldiers watched in silence.

I turned to Sandy. "Why did they do that?"

"He must have been caught stealing or gambling. Washington has forbidden throwing the dice here because it causes fights."

"So you think this fellow was gambling?"

"Perhaps. Actually, he's lucky. As an officer, he's merely cashiered, as you saw—disgraced and sent away. A regular soldier might have been whipped for such offenses."

In the weeks that followed, I witnessed many such whippings. They were common enough, for there were many offenses carrying such a penalty. Chief among them was desertion, but even such a small offense as failure to use the vaults—the latrine ditches—was punishable by five licks of the lash.

Just when everything looked the blackest, however, things changed for the better. The weather suddenly turned unseasonably warm, melting the two streams that converged near Washington's headquarters. The shad, gulled into thinking spring had arrived in February, started their run upstream to spawn.

Up the Schuylkill River came the fish, their silvery scales flashing in the sunlight. The men plunged into the water, shouting and laughing, pulling out writhing shad by handfuls, armfuls, and shirtfuls. Even the cavalry was called into action, riding horses back and forth across the shallows to herd the fish into the infantry's waiting hands.

I had a prodigious fine time, shucking off my shirt and jumping into the river, plucking the slippery-finned shad from the shallows and throwing them to Sandy on shore. I kept splashing and inviting him to join the fun, but he stubbornly refused, watching wistfully from the bank.

I never forgot the taste of that fresh fish, cooked over the fires that day: To me it tasted like hope. So did the rest of the food that came into camp, after the capable General Greene took over the task of finding supplies for the army.

At about the same time as the shad run, there was another welcome arrival—Baron William Augustus Henry von Steuben, a high-ranking Prussian officer sent by Benjamin Franklin to train the troops.

It was on the Grand Parade that I first saw the baron trying to teach a rudimentary drill to a gaggle of soldiers. The soldiers' clumsy mistakes were almost funny, but when I remembered how Brandywine had been lost because the Continentals couldn't maneuver quickly enough, the smile died on my face and I watched the man who hoped to change this.

He was no graceful youth like the redheaded Lafayette. If anything, the baron's big nose and apoplectic temper put me in mind of Squire Cheyney. As he watched the men colliding and dropping their muskets, he jumped up and down in a rage. Though I understood not a word of foreign tongues, it was easy to see that the words issuing from his lips were not flowery compliments.

"I wonder what that language is," I muttered.

"'Tis French—but the words are not familiar ones," Sandy unexpectedly replied. "Oh, wait—that I understood."

"What did he say?" I asked, stunned at Sandy's knowledge. Despite my mother's urgings, my book learning was all too meager. Even reading was too taxing to be pleasurable.

Sandy choked. "He . . . er . . . insulted their mothers."

"Where did you learn French?"

"My guardian hired good tutors."

"But why—," I started to ask, but Sandy shushed me and gestured toward the baron, whose face had grown as red as a beet while he bellowed at a slim young man hovering nervously at his side.

Sandy dragged me away so he could laugh aloud. "He told his aide to swear for him in English!" he gasped.

I joined Sandy's hilarity, but then asked a more serious question. "What's a boy like you—bred as a gentleman—doing out here at Valley Forge?"

"A boy like me?" he smiled. "I'm fighting for Independency."

I looked around at the peaceful scene. "But I don't see any fighting," I said with a shrug.

"Surely you are joking me, Geordie! Don't you see that keeping the army together is a great battle in itself? Why, I heard von Steuben say that no European army would stay together under such conditions." He gestured toward the men on the Grand Parade, who were laughing uproariously at the Prussian's fractured profanity. "But we've stayed. 'Tis one battle we've won," he said proudly.

"But that doesn't answer why you've made it your battle. You've no brother to care for here. Why have you left a life of comfort for firecakes and the itch?"

"I expect to make my own decisions and shoulder my own responsibilities when I am full grown. Why shouldn't my country be able to do the same?" His brown eyes glowed.

It was a simple statement, but it made more sense to me than all the high-flown sentences of the Declaration of Independence that had so infuriated my father. I solemnly took off my tricorne, took out the cockade hidden inside, and fastened it on the brim. Then another sudden burst of laughter from the men behind us drew our attention and we returned to watch the drill.

I don't know whether it was the translated profanity or the men's amusement upon hearing it that did the trick, but von Steuben's "school of the soldier" well-nigh transformed the Continental army. He simplified the commands and personally taught them to handpicked men, who went off to teach others. Between the fish in their bellies, the spring in the air, and their affection for this amusing foreigner, the men learned their paces apace. The whole camp was abuzz from sunup to sundown.

At last Will was able to leave the hut, leaning heavily on his old cane. Despite the happy occasion, he looked at me with a solemn expression. "Geordie, I thank you with all my heart for coming here to help.

Once again, you've saved my life. But now 'tis high time for you to leave."

"But I want to stay and help! I'm a patriot, too," I protested, pointing to his cockade on my hat.

"That's as may be, lad, but your duty lies at home. Mother needs you, and so does Father."

I fell silent, knowing he was in the right of it. I quickly gathered up my gear, but when I looked for Sandy to bid him farewell, he was nowhere to be found. Regretfully, I hid Will's cockade back inside my tricorne and set off for home.

Needless to say, Mother was pleased to have me at home again. 'Twas time for the spring grafting, one of Father's methods to improve his orchard beyond that of the ordinary farm. I drudged away in the orchard, sliding new cuttings under the bark of old branches and sealing them up with beeswax so the sap would run through the whole. I tried not to miss my brother and my friend—my well-educated friend, Sandy.

I was determined not to be such an unlettered numskull the next time we met. Mother was delighted when I asked that she tutor me in the evenings, especially when I studied so eagerly and progressed so far in only a couple of months.

Father made strides, too. Gradually his hearing, speech, and understanding were returning. This fact was obvious when he discovered that France had agreed to send troops and supplies to help the rebels. He worried over the broadening of the war, which caused the British to leave Philadelphia to consolidate their army in New York. He also derided the alliance itself, although not with the vigor of his previous wrath. Somehow his brush with death had mellowed his anger into sorrow.

"I simply cannot understand these rebels. Why, the French king is a true tyrant—his people have no rights at all! I'm sure France is only seeking to renew its old quarrels with England. When I think of Americans welcoming aid from our old enemy—those frogs we fought up and down our frontier—"

"Frogs?" I burst out.

Mother looked upset. "'Tis a most insulting term for the French because they eat frogs' legs, Geordie. Laban, thee knows such inhumane language distresses me."

"'Tis the French who are inhumane, Patience," Father said wearily. "Didn't they set the Indians against our settlers?" He leaned back against the pillows and sighed. "I don't know what's to become of us, compounding with French tyrants against people of our own blood."

Several days later, the Derrys came to visit Fa-

ther. He was so bored with his own company that he welcomed new faces, even those of neighbors with opposing politics. Besides, Father knew Master Derry had helped with the farmwork—though he didn't know how much, with me gone to Valley Forge. Therefore, Father swallowed his politics and greeted the Derrys with wary courtesy.

Almost as soon as they were in the chamber, Mistress Derry hissed at me with a conspiratorial air and slipped a paper into my hand. I glanced furtively at the red wax seal. It bore the familiar imprint of Will's signet ring.

Making some lame excuse, I ran out of the room and out of the house, not stopping until I reached the orchard. As I took the folded letter from my breeches pocket, I was glad I'd worked so hard on my reading. Turning the paper over, I saw my name written on the front in handwriting nothing like my own untidy scrawl. Surely, for all his tutoring, Sandy wouldn't form his letters so delicately, I thought, my forehead prickling with worry. Has something happened to Sandy so that a lady has had to write for him?

Ripping off the seal, I scanned the closely written sheets until I found the signature, Sandy, written in the same hand. With a soft whistle of relief and a grin at Sandy's overly elegant writing, I eagerly read his letter.

Dear Geordie,

How unhappy I was to find you gone when I
returned to Valley Forge, but after Will explained
he'd sent you home, I felt better. I thought you'd
like an account of happenings at Valley Forge and
Philadelphia.

First of all, and most important, was the arrival of the welcome news that France is now our
ally. When this was announced to the men, what
a huzzah went up! Then, later, we celebrated in
style, with a *feu de joie* ("fire of joy") of all the
guns in camp. How splendidly the men marched,
in all manner of formations, handling their muskets and bayonets as well as any redcoats I've seen
drilling in Philadelphia.

At the end, everyone shouted "Long live the
king of France" and "Long live the American
states." There was thunderous applause and
shouts, and thousands of hats sailed into the air.
How they found their owners again I cannot say.

Soon after, I had to return to the city. There I
was a witness to a very different kind of celebration: a huge party for General Howe, about to be
sent back to England. I thought it a shame to

waste so much money on foolish pleasure, but the Philadelphia belles had no such qualms. I saw them flirting and dancing with the British officers without a care in the world.

The very morning after the party, Howe attacked an American detachment led by Lafayette at Barren Hill, overlooking the Schuylkill. Howe was so certain he'd capture Lafayette that before he left, he invited friends to dinner to meet "the Boy." Alas for the general's dinner plans: By some very tricky marching, Lafayette was able to escape down a path to the river with all his men. For this we can bless the baron for his good work—and bad language.

A funny story is told of Barren Hill, though I know not if 'tis true. Some bear-helmeted British grenadiers, newly arrived from England, went with Howe and happened to encounter a small band of Algonquian Indians marching with Lafayette who were in full Indian battle gear, war paint and all. Rumor says that when the Indians and the grenadiers suddenly came face-to-face in the skirmish, the bizarre appearance of each side sent the other scurrying!

I have one more interesting bit of news— about our friend Ned Owens. Remember how upset he was when Conway was deposed? Well, he now has a new idol, the hero of Saratoga, Benedict Arnold. After the British left Philadelphia, General Washington made Arnold the military governor of the city. Whatever respect I had for Arnold was shattered by his infatuation for that loyalist snippet, Peggy Shippen. But, as the witcrackers say, "That's another Tory."

In truth, now that both armies are gone (and hundreds of city loyalists have fled to New York), I find my regular life decidedly flat.

I hope this letter finds your father on the mend and your mother in good spirits. You may inform her that the last time I saw Billy, he was dressed in an elegant new uniform and mounted on a steed far better than Buttercup. His limp has never left him, but as he can still ride, he's to be a cavalry "pioneer"—a scout for the army. I pray he comes through this murderous war with no further injuries or fevers.

Your obedient servant,
Sandy

After I finished reading Sandy's letter, I looked again at the handwriting of the letter, chuckling to

myself that I had thought it written by a lady. How
Sandy would laugh when I told him of my mistake!
But then I realized I might never have the chance to
tease him. I didn't even know his real name. Sandy
could be short for Alexander *or it could just refer to*
his sand-colored hair. His given name could be alto-
gether different, and he had never told me his family
name. Without either, how could I ever hope to find
such a slip of a lad in the big city of Philadelphia?

Suddenly Geordie stopped. "Someone's coming,"
he said, jumping to his feet.

I could hear the sound of the car coming up
the driveway. "Don't go yet. Tell me, did you ever
find Sandy?"

The kitchen door slammed. "Lars, I'm home!"
Mom called to me. "I'll bring your penicillin up in a
second."

I looked back toward Geordie, but, as always
when my parents showed up, my friendly shade
had disappeared.

My mother walked into my room, shaking the
penicillin bottle. "Hi, honey, how do you feel?" she
asked sympathetically.

"Just putrid," I said, smiling at my secret joke.
She poured out a spoonful of the pink medicine.

When I swallowed it without making a face, she looked at me closely. "What's this—none of the usual complaints about how awful it tastes?"

"Oh, it's not so bad," I said aloud. *Compared to leeches,* I thought with a shudder.

"You must *really* be sick, honey," she said, feeling my forehead. "Is there anything you feel like eating? Soda pop? Chicken soup?"

There was something I felt like eating, but it was neither of those.

"Got any applesauce?" I asked.

14

Where There's a Will

Dad put down his coffee cup and sent a disbelieving look across the breakfast table. "I never thought I'd hear you actually *plead* to go to school, Lars!"

"But we're setting up for Colonial Day. It's on Monday."

"Colonial Day?" Dad looked puzzled.

Mom clicked her tongue. "He told you about it, Erik. It's a colonial reenactment thing. The kids are even supposed to go by a colonial name—to help them get the feel of the era."

"What name are you going to use, Lars?" Dad asked, picking up his cup again. "*Ebenezer,* like Judge Bank?"

"I know!" Mom chimed in. "How about *George*—your ancestor's name and your middle name, as Aunt Cass kept reminding us."

Dad scoffed. "That's not old-fashioned enough. Now, how about *Ezekiel*—sounds like a big wheel— or *Ichabod,* as in *Crane.*"

"What about *George,* as in *Washington?*" Mom retorted.

"For Pete's sake, you guys, give me a break!" I broke in, laughing. "I'll think of something."

"*Pete*—now *there's* a good name," Mom mused. "Reminds me that we ought to give your brother a call."

"Poor Peter," I said. "He missed out on a lot, having to stay in Minnesota. Aunt Cass, and . . . and everything."

Mom came over and gave me a hug. "I just had to do that. I'm so proud of you, Lars," she said.

"Seems like a couple of centuries ago you arrived here, L. George. You've grown up a lot since then." Dad cleared his throat. "So what else is going to happen at this Colonial Day?"

"Oh, crafts and stuff," I replied. "And by the way, we're having a museum at school, Mom. Can I take the riddle?"

"The what? Oh, you mean that old sieve. Sure, you can take whatever you want. Too bad we can't find the cup and ball—that would be a nice museum piece." Mom paused, then with a wry smile added, "Be nice to find the will, too."

My face must have mirrored my worry about the missing will, because after a quick glance at me, Mom went on, "Cheer up, Lars! By tomorrow you won't be contagious anymore and maybe you'll feel up to going out."

"Could we go to Valley Forge?" I asked eagerly. "I feel fine!"

"Sure—call up a friend."

My eagerness faded some. "I don't know anybody's number."

"We know Pat's. Look, I'll call her up and see if she'd like to go to Valley Forge with you tomorrow," Mom said.

I regarded this plan with mixed feelings, but Mom soon came back to report that it was all set.

"And guess what?" she added. "Pat's going to pick you up on her horse! There are riding trails at Valley Forge."

"Horseback? Geez, I don't know." I remembered how I had disgraced myself at camp. Still, riding to Valley Forge sounded like fun. I hoped I could stay in the saddle that far.

Saturday morning turned out to be bright,

sunny, and unseasonably warm. As I waited outside for Pat, I remembered how Aunt Cass had bamboozled me into thinking Pat was a boy. I was still smiling at this memory when Pat came cantering up the drive. Her white horse had unexpectedly blue eyes. To cover up the awkwardness I felt, I asked Pat about them.

She laughed. "In a horse, they're called *glass eyes*. Dad got her for me because he said blue eyes run in our family. Except for me—I guess I got brown eyes from that great-great-whatever-grammy whose picture is on my wall. Dad says I take after her—that we're as alike as two peas in a pod."

I made a face. "Please—don't mention peas."

"Oh, you hate them too? Well, I hate to tell you, but we grow bumper crops of them in our garden—so did Cass."

"I know, I know."

Mom brought out a brown paper bag. "A snack," she said.

I took it from her and peeked inside. "Oh, good—pasties!"

"Aunt Cass used to make those for me," Pat said. "I haven't had any since she died."

"These are from her recipe," Mom said. "I'll give you a copy if you like—to remember her by."

I handed Pat the bag and gingerly climbed up behind her.

"Take it easy," Mom said. "Lars isn't much of a horseman."

"Don't worry, Mrs. Olafson, I'm a careful driver," Pat joked, and chirruped the horse down the drive.

At first as we jounced along Seek-No-Further Pike I was too nervous to say much. Then Pat told me it was a family tradition to name horses after flowers, so her mare was called Petunia. It seemed silly to be intimidated by a horse named Petunia, and soon Pat and I were talking about all kinds of things—Pat pointing out the sights, and me telling her some of the Valley Forge stuff I'd picked up from Geordie. Of course I didn't reveal my source of information. As we talked, I was more and more tempted to tell her my secret, but how could I explain without her thinking I was either lying or crazy?

Finally I said, a little stiffly, "You know, before we got to Penncroft Farm, Mom kidded around about it being haunted."

Pat replied, "Yeah, Aunt Cass hinted about that once in a while. Of course, she loved to bamboozle kids."

"I know, I know," I said, laughing a little nervously.

Pat went on, "I could almost believe it is haunted sometimes, especially…"

Petunia, startled by a passing car, jumped sideways, and for a little while we were too busy holding on to talk.

After the horse settled back into her easy gait, I took up the subject again, as casually as I could. "What were you saying about almost believing Penncroft is haunted, especially…?"

Pat chuckled. "Oh, yes—especially when Cass played that creepy Captain Nemo piece on her organ. With the stops pulled out and the wind right, we could hear it at Blackberry Hill. Okay, Lars, here's the turnoff for the park. I just love this part— going through the covered bridge over Valley Creek."

Must be new, I thought, remembering that Geordie and Sandy had forded the creek. Then, as we clattered over the bridge, I couldn't help comparing it with the other one, where I'd first seen Geordie. The thought gave me the nerve to blurt out, "Pat, do you believe in ghosts?"

"When I come to Valley Forge, I do a little. There's something special about a spot where real people suffered and died. Not ghosts exactly—just a feeling. And about three thousand of the people who camped here with Washington died."

I thought about Will, and how close he'd come to death, and felt too much to speak.

As we wound our way up the long hill to the right, Pat said over her shoulder, "Now, look, Lars—don't expect this to be very dramatic. There wasn't any battle fought here, you know. Lots of people are disappointed when they find that out."

"But there was a battle," I said. "Just keeping the army together for the whole winter was a battle. Hey, look—there are some of the huts! I can't believe they're still here!"

"Hate to tell you, Lars, but they're all reconstructions," she said apologetically. "These huts are supposed to be where Wayne's brigade was. Those were guys from Pennsylvania."

"I knew that," I said as if joking, though underneath I was feeling more and more excited. "Let's stop and take a look." We slid off Petunia and tied her up, then went into one of the huts. It was so like what Geordie had described that I could almost see Will lying on the rough bunk, shivering on filthy straw.

Pat looked at me curiously. "See any ghosts in here, Lars?"

A shudder ran over me. "Sort of. Memories, anyway."

"Memories? I thought you'd never been here before."

"Let's go to the museum," I said hastily.

We climbed back on Petunia and trotted along the road that marked the outer defenses. As we went, I suddenly had the oddest feeling that Petunia was following Buttercup's hoofprints, carrying Geordie and Sandy to Valley Forge to help Will.

Parking Petunia below the museum, we went inside. There we found display cases full of artifacts from the Revolution, like the ones at the Brandywine museum. Of course, Pat had been there so much she had favorite things to show me and lots to say, especially about what women did at Valley Forge.

"Yup, not only did Mrs. Washington and other officers' wives come here, but so did lots of other women whose husbands were here. They nursed the sick, washed clothes, and cooked. I wonder if our ancestors were here, too."

"I doubt it. In his portrait, old George looks like a guy who wouldn't do anything that would mess up his ruffled shirt."

Pat indignantly started to argue, but another exhibit caught her eye. "I never noticed this display before. It's about that German guy, von Steuben, who taught the Americans to march and maneuver. Apparently he was a phony: Instead of being some big shot with the Prussian army, he was really only a captain and hadn't done any soldiering for years. And get this—it says that Ben Franklin helped fake the guy's papers so Congress would accept his help!"

"Let me see that!" I leaned over to read the text aloud. *"His title was false but his skill was not.* That's funny," I muttered. "He never said anything about a phony title!"

"Who?" Pat asked, giving me a quizzical look.

"Huh? Oh, nothing." I quickly turned back to the display and read on. *"So at the end of the winter at Valley Forge, the Americans had well-trained soldiers and official French support. It made all the difference."* Uneasy that I had said too much, I went over to another case and peered at its contents.

Pat came up beside me. "Look at those," she said, pointing at some leaden dice. "They must have gambled to pass the time."

"Oh, no—that was against Washington's rules," I muttered, remembering the backs striped in punishment for gambling.

"Well, looks like *somebody* was breaking the rules," Pat said. Then she read, *"Failure to use the vaults will be punished by five lashes.* What the heck does that mean?"

"The vaults were the latrines," I whispered, blushing.

Pat looked at me with new respect, mixed with embarrassment. "How do you know all this stuff? You know what? I think you're a phony yourself, L. George Olafson."

"A phony?" I echoed weakly.

Pat grinned. "Aunt Cass told me she'd heard you were terrible at history—not the least bit interested. And all the time you were as crazy about history as I am. You phony!"

"Well, not quite *all* the time," I admitted modestly, grinning back at her. Suddenly it seemed okay that she wasn't a Patrick.

We climbed back on Petunia "in perfect charity with one another," as Geordie would say, and rode across the Grand Parade to Washington's headquarters. There I saw the woefully short bed upon which the tall general had slept sitting up. And there I could almost see Sandy holding yarn for Lady Washington to wind.

"Lapdog," I muttered.

214

"Huh?"

"Oh, nothing. Hey—want to skip rocks?"

"Ducks and drakes?" she teased. "Sure."

We went down to the river. This time I did out-skip her, and soon I was telling her all about the shad run up the Schuylkill that had helped feed the soldiers. Luckily, instead of piquing her curiosity, it whetted her appetite.

"I'm starving—just like the previous visitors. Though I shouldn't really joke about it, I suppose. Sounds pretty awful."

"Come on, let's eat those pasties," I said.

After we wolfed down the pasties, we heard some carillon bells. Pat said they were from the Washington Memorial Chapel, and we rode up to investigate. The music was over by the time we arrived, but we decided to look around anyway. As we started down the hallway of the chapel, a familiar voice made me grab Pat's hand and pull her behind a column.

"Lars, what are you doing?" she spluttered.

"It's Mr. Owens," I hissed. We peeked around the column.

He was standing just inside the entrance to a small private museum. In his arms was a large green drum with a gold eagle painted on the side.

"I'm sorry to take back my ancestor's drum after it's been here so long," Mr. Owens was saying, "but I'll be opening my own museum soon so I must get everything together."

"Thanks for the loan. It's been a pleasure to exhibit a drum that was actually used here at Valley Forge," said his companion.

Mr. Owens seemed to get a little taller. "Oh yes, my ancestor was right here—starving and freezing with the rest of the army. He also warned Washington at Brandywine, you know."

Pat nudged me. "Gosh, Eddie was right. I thought that was just one of his tall tales," she whispered.

"Shhh," I said. I peered back around the arch, then ducked back again out of sight just as Mr. Owens swept by. After he was gone, we went back to where Petunia was calmly munching away at the dry yellow grass within her reach.

"I didn't know Mr. Owens had a museum," Pat said, making a face. "I hope we don't have to go *there* on a field trip. I couldn't stand Eddie's bragging."

"He doesn't have one—yet. And won't if I can help it," I declared. I suddenly felt exhausted and asked Pat if we could go home. Soon we were clip-clopping back on the pike.

"Mom told me about the missing will," Pat said sympathetically. "I'll help you look for it if you like."

"Thanks, but we've already looked every-where."

"Oh," she said sadly. We went along in silence for a while, the only sounds coming from Petunia as she ambled along. Then, in rhythm with Petunia's gait, Pat started to sing.

> *Come, bridle me, my milk-white steed,*
> *Come, bridle me, my pony,*
> *That I may ride to fair London town*
> *To plead for my Geordie.*

"G-geordie?" I stammered, interrupting her song.

"It's just a folk song Dad learned when he was a kid. He said it was an old family favorite—prob-ably because of our ancestor. *Geordie*'s a nickname for *George,* you know. Geordie Hargreaves was the guy whose picture is in your room. It's his wife—our great-some-thing-grammy—whose portrait Aunt Cass gave me. Want to stop and see it?"

I mumbled some kind of agreement. It was as if there were lots of puzzle pieces swirling around in my brain that I couldn't fit together. Meanwhile, Pat went on singing.

I wish I were in yonder grove
Where times I have been many
With my broad sword and my pistol, too,
I'd fight for the life of Geordie.

By the time we reached Blackberry Hill Farm and climbed up to Pat's room, I was beginning to understand. Still, it was something of a shock to see the woman in the portrait, with her mischievous brown eyes, a feathered hat perched askew on her sand-colored hair. I looked down at the metal plate and read the inscription aloud. "'Cassandra Hargreaves, painted by Charles Willson Peale, Philadelphia, 1805.'"

"Of course," Pat said offhandedly, "you must have known there was a Cassandra in the family tree somewhere. Both Aunt Cass and your mother were named after her. And I might as well tell you that Cassandra is my middle name. According to family tradition she was quite a tomboy—they called it *hoyden* in her day—and a kind of under-cover spy for Washington."

"Way undercover," I repeated slowly. Sandy, with the tricorne always askew. Little, plucky Sandy had somehow become my great-great-great-something-grandmother. And Pat's.

"You do look like her, Pat," I said, still in shock.

"Alike as two peas," she chuckled. "As long as I'm showing you family relics, I might as well show you this, too." She pulled out the ring on the chain around her neck that I'd seen her toy with when we'd first met. "See, there's a motto engraved in-side: 'Ubi Voluntas Via Ibi Est.' I think it means . . ."

"'Where there's a will, there's a way,'" I chimed in.

Her eyes widened in amazement. "My gosh, do you know Latin?"

"No, just that phrase. I, ah, heard it's our family motto."

"Yup. 'Where there's a will—'" She stopped suddenly. "Wait a minute! About that will of Aunt Cass's. I just remembered something. When I was little, Cass used to play hide-and-seek with me. One time I peeked through my fingers and saw her go into the barn, but when I went in there, I couldn't find her anywhere. Finally I gave up, went outside, and yelled, 'Allee allee all in free.' I peeked again and saw her come out of that barn. I couldn't figure it out, but now I wonder if there might be some kind of secret room in there!"

Suddenly all the puzzle pieces fell into place. I shouted, "Grampa's Folly!" and gave Pat a big hug.

She looked at me as if I had suddenly sprouted another head. "You feeling all right, Lars?" she squeaked.

"Patience—you're the one who's a genius! That's it! Come on— I think I know where there *is* a will."

"You know where it is? Come on, Lars, tell me!"

"No way!" I said, grinning from ear to ear.

We ran outside and jumped onto Petunia. I urged Pat to go faster and faster, until we were flying over the field. I felt like echoing Washington's shout at Brandywine, "Push along, old man, push along!"

As we thundered up the driveway, Mom came rushing out of the house. When she saw our excited faces, she gave a sigh of relief. "Good grief— I thought you'd been thrown off that horse, or that it had run away with you."

I jumped down and ran over to her, Pat at my heels. "Mom, Mom!" I burst out, so breathless from excitement that my words came out in gasps. "I think I've got it! Tell me what Aunt Cass said in the hospital. Her message for me. Her exact words."

Mom frowned in an effort to remember. "Let's see now. She said something about a riddle and taking you down a peg. I thought she meant your setting aside your pride and wearing a costume for her. I don't know—it didn't make sense."

"It does to me!" I shouted. Without another word, I sprinted for the barn. Just as I had done the first time, I groped along the wall. This time I knew what I was looking for: the large wooden peg on which the riddle had hung. I gripped the peg firmly and help my breath.

Just then, Mom and Pat came up behind me. "What on *earth* are you doing, Lars?" Mom said, panting from her sprint.

"This is where the riddle was hanging. Aunt Cass was trying to tell me to pull down the peg where I had found the riddle."

I pulled down as hard as I could. A dreadful groan filled the barn.

"Yipes, my brother was right: This place *is* haunted," Mom said, laughing nervously.

"That's no ghost moaning," I said. "Just take a look." I found the cord for the light and tugged it.

There was a gaping hole where the peg had been—a hole large enough for a person to crawl through. To hide from Indian raids that never came. Or to hide from Tory fathers.

Mom flew into action. "Quick, Lars, get the flashlight!"

I ran to the kitchen as though pursued by Indians or Tories, grabbed a couple of flashlights, and tore back to the barn. My heart was thumping so loud I could hear it as I shined the light into the hole and the three of us crawled inside.

Mom exclaimed, "Look! There's the cup and ball!"

"And here," I said triumphantly, reaching for a yellow legal pad, "is Aunt Cass's final will."

Mom took the will from me with shaking hands and went out into the sunlight to read it. I followed her, while Pat stayed tactfully behind.

For several long minutes, I watched Mom read in silence. Finally, she looked up. "Why, Aunt Cass *didn't* leave Penncroft Farm to me!" she exclaimed.

So Aunt Cass had left the farm to Eddie Owens's father after all. I felt like throwing up. Stricken, I looked at my mother and was shocked by her broad smile.

"She left it to *you!*" she laughed, flinging her arms around me. Then she read through the rest of the will. "She says she wanted to make sure you appreciated the farm, and that if you found this, it proved you had been guided by the proper spirit."

Hearing this, I choked. "Boy, this dust is awful." I coughed on purpose a couple of times.

"You really were one smart cookie to find that secret door! How did you know about it, anyway?"

That was the question I was afraid she might ask. "Well, ah, Patience told me..." Just then, Pat came out of the barn with an open book in her hand, so I quickly changed the subject. "Uh, Mom, so what does the will say about the Owenses? Did she leave something to them?"

"I can't figure this out, exactly. Something about some memoirs. She says they now belong to you, Lars (she calls you *L. George*), but that Edward Owens IX (look how fancy she wrote it—no wonder it caught Ellen Hargreaves's attention) may use them for historic documentation if he feels the world is ready for an accurate account of his ancestors. And..." She flipped over to the second page and hurriedly scanned its contents. "No, that's all she said about any of the Owenses."

Pat held up the book she'd brought out. "This must be what she meant by memoirs. There's a whole pile of 'em in there. And look what it says about Edward Owens!" she crowed.

We clustered around Pat and read the faded, spidery writing in the musty leather volume.

15

Riddles Revealed

In the spring of 1778, after the British left Philadelphia with the Americans right behind them, we settled back into an almost normal existence at Penncroft Farm. Still, I hungrily followed the course of the struggle. It was from Mistress Derry that I heard about Benedict Arnold's treason, though her account was garbled by comments about Peggy Shippen Arnold and her lamentable taste in clothes. Eventually I sifted out the important facts of the matter: how Arnold had bargained with the new British commander, General Clinton, to allow West Point, the crucial fortress under his command, to fall to the enemy. I wondered if Will was one of the soldiers whose lives Arnold had been willing to sacrifice for British gold, and I thanked God the plot had been discovered before anyone died to satisfy Arnold's ambitions. I also wondered

if Ned Owens had found a new idol. Between the dis-
graced Conway and the treacherous Arnold, Ned had
been unlucky in his choices.

Meanwhile, by great good fortune and sheer grit,
Father regained much of his former strength, though
he was never again as vigorous as before. Mother and
I, fearing to provoke him, never told him of the letters
we received from Will, who seemed to be thriving as
a cavalry pioneer. Sometimes the sorrowful look in
his eye made me think he wanted to ask about Will,
but he never did. Not once through those long, long
years of war.

During those years, I grew to a man's height, tow-
ering over my mother and approaching my father's
stature. Many times I thought of leaving to join the
Continental forces, but I knew my mother couldn't
have borne it, and my father truly needed me at Penn-
croft Farm. Still, I missed my brother mighty sorely
and chafed to be a part of it all. My heart was with the
Continentals, now in the South, where the British
had taken the war, again, in hopes of loyalist support.

What they found instead was the great defeat at
Yorktown, Virginia, where the British commander
Lord Cornwallis surrendered his entire army. The
war was as good as over—or so we thought.

When the news arrived of the American victory,

we heard there was to be a great illumination in the city of Philadelphia. Fireworks were to light up the skies and everyone was to place a lit candle in their windows. Needless to say, at Penncroft Farm there were no celebratory candles alight. In unspoken agreement, Father, Mother, and I went to bed early.

We were all asleep when we were awakened by the rumbling of men's voices. I joined my parents in their bedchamber, which faced the front of the house. Through the window we saw a half-score of men, their faces distorted by hatred and by the flickering light of the torches they bore.

My father, undaunted, threw up the window sash and shouted, "What do you want here?"

"Why is your house not lit for the great victory?"

"'Tis a victory that gives me no joy," Father replied.

"Only traitors talk like that. I say let's burn him out!" A hoarse chorus of ayes greeted this cry.

"Father!" I whispered urgently. "Tell them you've a son with the Continentals. They won't destroy a patriot soldier's home!"

"I cannot shelter behind Will after all that's happened."

My mother gasped. "Look! They're torching the barn!"

For a moment we watched helplessly as flames engulfed the dry wood siding of the barn, the roar of the fire drowning out the men's blood-chilling hurrays. Then I flew down the stairs and out to the barn, yelling for them to stop. I might as well have whispered for all they heard of my cry.

I blindly thrashed about until I grabbed the arm of one of them, and was shocked to find it belonged to someone I had seen before. He was taller, but the shape was the same. It was Ned Owens.

I shouted, "Ned! What are you doing with this lot?"

"Hush! We're not to use names," he hissed.

"This is my home! You know I'm not a Tory. You saw me at Brandywine, at Valley Forge with my brother. Tell them!"

Owens shrugged. "How do I know what you were doing? Perhaps you were a British spy." He shoved me aside and threw his torch into the haystack that leaned against the barn.

Suddenly hoofbeats clattered on the lane. A single horse cantered up. With eyes wild at the sight of the flames, it reared, hooves slicing at the smoky air. The two riders managed to slide off the horse's back unhurt. For the moment, I had eyes only for the taller of the two. It was Will, dressed from head to toe as a Continental cavalryman. In his hand was his old hand-carved cane, which he brandished over his head in fury as he shouted at the mob. "Shame, shame on you all! Is this how we are to build a new nation? By burning one another's homes?" Under his torrent of scathing words, the rampaging mob rapidly dwindled into a knot of ten chastened men.

Will, seeing this, called out to me. "There are buckets in the lean-to. Geordie, show them where. We must make a bucket chain to the pond."

In a daze, I joined the others; we worked like furies to quench the fire. It was only when the last flame was doused that I had the opportunity to look at Will's companion, a young lady dressed in an apple-green silken gown, with hair the color of golden sand and brown eyes full of mischief. There was something very familiar about this pretty girl, though I was sure I had never met her.

Then she spoke my name, and there was no mistaking her voice. And if that wasn't enough to convince me, the signet ring suspended from her necklace chain was. The girl was Sandy.

At my dumbfounded expression, she smiled.

I stood there as if struck by lightning. How could I have been such a sapskull? How had I been so bamboozled, so blind? How could I ever have believed

Sandy a boy? And why was it so much easier to know what to say to a scruffy little comrade than to this silken-gowned stranger?

I stuttered. "Wh-why the masquerade?"

She smiled at my astonishment. "Forgive my gulling you, Geordie, but I couldn't risk anyone's knowing who I was. You see, my guardian pretended to be a loyalist whilst the British held the city. He was a very high-placed gentleman who used his position to mingle with the British commanding officers. Everything he learned, he sent through me to Washington.

"We deemed it best that I pass as a boy, 'twas far safer. And then, later, I couldn't tell anyone what I had done, else my reputation would be in shreds." She laughed—a high, girlish laugh that I remembered very well.

"Only Billy here twigged my disguise," she went on, taking Will's hand affectionately. "When he heard my guardian had died, leaving me without family, he came to get me. He says he wants..." She stopped and looked uncertainly up at Will.

My brother put his arm around her and appealed to my parents, who had come out of the house. "You've always wanted a daughter. I hope Cassandra can stay and be my little sister."

In that instant I knew Cassandra would never be a sister to me.

My mother's only answer to Will's appeal was to enfold Sandy in her arms. Without releasing the girl, she turned to my father.

"Laban?" she whispered.

My father stood there in silence. We all waited, taut as fiddle strings, watching him. At last he spoke.

"Well, Patience, I judge that if Cornwallis can surrender his entire army, I can make peace with my own family—my two brave sons and my brave new daughter." A smile spread across his face—the first real smile I'd seen upon his countenance for all the long, weary years of war.

The next thing I knew, we were all standing in the mud hugging and crying and bussing one another. And we were a family again. A new family in a new nation. It felt grand.

I shut the book and cradled it in my hands. It was all there—all of Geordie's stories about Brandywine, Philadelphia, Whitemarsh, Valley Forge, and Penncroft Farm. And the other volumes promised to reveal even more than Geordie had told me. I looked up to find Mom and Pat staring at me.

"Are you all right, honey?" Mom asked. "You

look a little pale. Maybe you did too much after being sick. Why don't you lie down while I call Dad and tell him about finding the will?"

"I'm going straight home to tell my folks," Pat said.

"Yeah, that sounds like a good idea," I said faintly. "Bye, Pat. See you at Colonial Day."

"Right. Oh, boy, I can hardly wait to see how Eddie takes all this documentary proof about his ancestors' brave deeds in the Revolution," she said with a laugh.

After I watched Pat ride away, I ran back to the barn instead of heading for my bedroom. On the way I passed the wagon—the same rig Geordie had driven full of perry and apples, and I had driven down our driveway. I touched it as if in a dream, then made my way into Grampa's Folly, where I spoke sternly into the empty room.

"George Hargreaves, I want a word with you." I stopped and listened, but there was no sound. "George Hargreaves? George? Oh, c'mon, Geordie, I know you're here somewhere!" I exclaimed.

"No need to bluster so rudely, Lars. Of course I'm here."

Geordie climbed through the opening from the main part of the barn. He was tossing his tricorne up and down nonchalantly. "Want to play huzzle-cap?" he inquired, as if nothing had changed.

"Huzzlecap! You . . . you ninnyhammer, you sap-skull, you great booby, you . . . you . . ." I ran out of eighteenth-century insults and ended lamely, "Why didn't you tell me?"

Geordie shrugged. "I did, after a fashion."

"B-but how come you don't look like the portrait? Why are you just a kid?"

"I judged 'twould be easier for you to talk with somebody near your own age. So, that's the age I picked for this . . . ah . . . visit. And now that you've solved this little riddle, you can carry on at Penn-croft Farm and I can take a rest."

"What?"

Geordie looked at me a little sadly. "Well, yes, it's your turn to look after things here. Besides, now you have begun to make friends—*real* friends, not paltry shades. You don't need me anymore."

"But, Geordie, I . . ."

"Don't fret, Lars. You'll find that you truly *don't* need me around anymore."

"But . . ."

"Farewell."

"Geordie!" I cried out. But my shade had gone. I was alone in the barn. I picked up the book again and tried to console myself with Geordie's faded words, but I missed the writer of those words "mighty sorely," as he would have said.

The sadness of Geordie's farewell stayed with me all that weekend. Even when Judge Bank examined the will and pronounced it valid, I couldn't get too enthusiastic. It wasn't until Monday, Colonial Day, that I began to feel better.

Winning so many of the colonial competitions helped a lot. So did the colonial name tag I had pinned on my waistcoat. With secret satisfaction I looked down at it and read it to myself. There, in my best calligraphy, was the name *Geordie.*

My mother came hustling up to me, with Dad trailing along in her wake. "Good grief, Lars, that's the third blue ribbon you've won today!" she exclaimed. "How did you learn to be so good at old stuff like that game with the funny name—huzzle-cap? You got every penny—pardon me, I mean *farthing,* in that three-cornered hat," Mom exclaimed.

"Beginner's luck," I said, thinking of the time I had spent pitching coins into Geordie's tricorne.

Dad looked around at the mob of children and parents nearby spinning wool, making butter and paper, smithing tin. "This Colonial Day is certainly a good idea for you kids. I'm even learning a thing or two myself—like about that cider press. Will Hargreaves said he'd show me how to build one."

Mom clapped her hands. "Won't it be fun to make some apple cider at Penncroft just like they used to?"

"Or perry," I said, hastily adding, "That is, er, *very* . . . very fun."

"Pat—er, *Patience* Hargreaves's song about 'Geordie' was so touching," Mom said. "I'd be flattered if I were you, 'L. Geordie.'"

Mrs. Hettrick joined us, looking as much like Martha Washington as she could in a white yarn wig. "Welcome to the colonies," she said, making a deep curtsy. "I'm Mistress Hettrick."

My father bowed. "Nice to meet you, madam. You've really sparked Lars's interest in history."

Mrs. Hettrick waved away the compliment. "Oh, but I haven't done anything out of the ordinary! I thought you two must be giving him extra help at home."

"No, nothing special," Mom said, looking a little puzzled.

"It must have been those fantastic memoirs that piqued his interest—like that terrific account of your ancestor at the Battle of Brandywine. Yes, Lars—that is"—Mrs. Hettrick peered at my name tag—"*Geordie*—learned a lot from those memoirs! He's the one who suggested making the hay labyrinth out by the obstacle course. It's incredible what he's picked up in such a short time."

"Yes, it is incredible," Mom said, glancing at me.

Mrs. Hettrick went on, "And I think it's simply marvelous that Lars is starting his own little museum in your barn. Such a clever name, too: The Museum of the First American Civil War. Nice of you to lend so many things for Colonial Day. The cup and ball and the cockade and that . . . what is it called, that sieve thing?"

"It's a riddle to me," I said, with a wide grin.

"Oh yes, a *riddle*. And everyone is buzzing about how you solved the mystery and found the will in that secret room. You know, Patience Hargreaves has been telling everybody what a Sherlock Holmes you were. You're quite the hero of the day."

"Not with everybody," I said, catching sight of Eddie Owens, whose face registered something close to misery. "I'll meet you in the gym, Mom. I've got to talk to someone."

I waded through the crowd and sat down next to Eddie.

"Hi, Ned," I said, reading his name tag.

He sighed. "Dad made me use *Ned*. How embarrassing!"

"Look, Eddie," I said earnestly, "It doesn't make any difference what your ancestors did, or what my ancestors did. What's important is what *we* are, and what *we* do."

Eddie sat up a little straighter. "But I told everybody my ancestor was a hero and now they think I'm a liar."

I stood up. "No, they've only found out that it's not so easy to know what happened in the past. And that things were just as messed up and confused back then as they are now."

Eddie looked down at the fake buckles flopping on his tennis shoes. One of his kneesocks was sagging around his ankle. He pulled up his sock, which drooped again as soon as he let go.

"Maybe you're right," he said with a half smile, which turned into a whole smile when I asked if he wanted to walk down to the gym with me, where the Virginia reel was about to begin.

We made our way to the gym. I felt a little nervous, but I knew what to do when I got there. Scanning the flock of costumed girls, I found the one I was looking for—a tall girl with mischievous brown eyes and sandy-colored hair.

I made an awkward little bow in front of her, as we were supposed to when asking someone to dance the Virginia reel.

"Hullo, uh, Geordie," she said self-consciously.

"Hullo, Patience," I said, nodding at her name tag. "It's a nice name, *Patience*. You shouldn't be ashamed of it."

"I guess I'm not anymore." Smiling, she held out her hand.

As we took our places for the dance, the girls in the opposite line fluttered like a row of butterflies. I had to admit to myself that they looked...well, at least interesting in their long skirts and mobcaps. Curious to see if the line of boys was equally impressive, I glanced down to my right.

Yes, I thought, *we boys look pretty authentic, too.* Like me, they all had pants tucked into knee-socks to resemble breeches, neatly tied neck cloths, and black three-cornered hats made of construction paper. One boy had even managed to get a real tricorne, I noticed. Then he turned and I saw his face.

It was Geordie. Catching my astonished eye, he gave an impish wink and bowed deeply to his partner. She was a slender girl with hair the same color as Pat's, wearing an apple-green silken gown.

I was so flustered that when the lively music began (on a most uncolonial record player), I completely forgot to dance.

"Lars, what are you doing? Do-si-do!" Pat squeaked, with laughing impatience that belied her name.

"Your servant, madam," I whispered, and concentrated on my steps for a moment. When I looked back down the line, Geordie and Cassandra were lost from sight in the swirl of costumed dancers.

Afterword

Whenever I read a partly made up, partly true story, I always want to know which part is which. Assuming that readers of this book might want to know this, too, I'll try to sort it out. Readers should remember, however, what Lars said about the past: "It's not so easy to know what happened...things were just as messed up and confused back then as they are now..."

Everything that happens in the historical part of this book is as true as I could make it, except for the insertion of Geordie (along with his family, Sandy, the Derrys, and the Owenses) and minor liberties taken with the sequence of Revolutionary events and with George Washington's wig (he didn't wear one). In addition to the famous (and infamous) figures of the Revolution, many other minor characters are based on actual people or events involving people whose names have faded into the past. For example, a Squire Cheyney tried to warn Washington, who was then reluctantly guided by Mr. Brown. American vedettes were surprised at Welsh's tavern and had to escape on foot. Quakers carried on their regular worship service despite skirmishing outside Kennett Meetinghouse. The manager of the elegant City Tavern was a man named Daniel Smith (a Tory who left with the British). There really was an orderly book that may have helped alert the patriots about British plans to attack Whitemarsh. Philadelphia was despoiled, and American prisoners did shiver and starve in the State House. The men at Valley Forge chanted "No bread, no soldier" and joked in the face of terrible hardships while the Conway Cabal tried to get Congress to replace Washington with Gates. Spies for both sides passed back and forth between Valley Forge and British-occupied Philadelphia with astonishing ease. In addition, Sandy's letter refers to real events (although she's right to doubt the story about the Indians and the Grenadiers scaring each other off at Barren Hill).

My central aim in making up this story, however, was not to gather anecdotes about the Revolution but to show that it was, indeed, the First American Civil War. There were many people who felt the same way Geordie's parents did, and for excellent reasons. It has been said that of the people living in America at the time of the Revolution, nearly one-third were loyalist and one-third were neutral. This means only one-third were active patriots. Of these, some (like my made-up Mr. Owens and the regrettably real Benedict Arnold) embraced the Revolution for personal gain or ambition. Most patriots, however, were genuinely committed to winning freedom from England, or they would not have given up so much to achieve it. An understanding of the complexities, the risks, the terror, and the uncertainties faced by our forefathers helps us see how remarkable their achievement was. Yet they were only people, and if they could muddle through incredibly difficult times, so can we.

Penncroft Farm, Blackberry Hill Farm, and Seek-No-Further Pike cannot be found on any map. Geordie and his family lived only on these pages. But there were many families that were as divided as theirs, and there were many Tories who suffered worse fates than a partly burned barn. Most lost their property. Some lost their lives. All lost their homeland, either literally or figuratively. They were part of our national history and should be remembered. They were the losers in the First American Civil War. Thank goodness.

Glossary*

agog—in a state of excited eagerness
apoplectic—liable to have a stroke (apoplexy)
bedlamite—insane person (Bedlam was a British insane asylum)
benighted—stranded by nightfall
buff—tan in color, bare skin ("in the buff" means "naked")
bumpkin—a hick, an ignorant person
bussing—kissing
charity—good will, friendship
ciphering—arithmetic, writing in secret code
cockade—a leather hat ornament showing political loyalty

*Definitions adapted from standard dictionaries, the *O.E.D.*, Eric Partridge's *Dictionary of Slang and Unconventional English,* and from recent reissues of *Samuel Johnson's Dictionary* (1755), Noah Webster's *Compendious Dictionary of the English Language* (1806), and the *1811 Dictionary of the Vulgar Tongue* (Capt. Francis Grose).

Conestoga—A Pennsylvania Indian tribe

Continental—referred to the American continent, therefore applied to American soldiers, Congress, and paper money

crop—a small whip

dab hand—an expert

deucedly—extremely (used in mild oath)

doleful—unhappy

doodle—a fool

farthing—a small British coin, worth only half a *ha'penny*

fathom—to understand thoroughly

flying hospital—temporary hospital

fortnight—two weeks

furlong—about ⅛ of a mile (a standard plowed furrow length)

gaiters—covering for the lower part of the leg

gewgaws—trinkets, toys

gull—to fool

ha'penny—a coin worth half a penny

Hessian—person from Hesse, a kingdom of central Germany

hob—the shelf inside a fireplace for keeping food warm

hornbook—reading chart covered with thin layer of cow's horn

huzzlecap—game in which players throw coins into a hat

larder—food storage area

leading strings—a sort of leash for toddlers

leeching—putting leeches on the skin to suck out "bad" blood

linsey-woolsey—coarse cloth made of linen and wool fiber

lobsterbacks—red-uniformed British soldiers

loyalist—a person who was loyal to the King of England

mite—a little bit (also, a tiny insect, see *scabies*)

mobcap—a woman's loose cap

mollycoddle—baby, overprotect

mulled—heated and flavored with spices

nattered—chattered, complained

ninnyhammer—a stupid person

nunchion—snack, light lunch

orderly book—a book containing battle plans

pallet—a straw mattress

periwigged—wearing a wig

perry—pear cider, fermented so it contained alcohol

pioneer—army scout

pomace—crushed pulp of fruit pressed for juice

puddingheart—a fearful person, a scaredycat

puncheon—a rough wooden surface made of split logs

putrid—infected, rotten (modern slang: "yucky")

redcoat—a British soldier (the uniforms were red)

redoubt—ditch with dirt piled up to provide shelter from attack *riddle*—a word puzzle, a mystery, a coarse sieve

rucksack—backpack

rushlights—candles with wicks made of rushes (a grassy plant)

sapskull—a fool

scabies—a skin disease caused by mites burrowing into the skin and laying eggs, causing intense itching

score—twenty

shot—bill, account

sideboard—a piece of dining-room furniture

slugabed—lazy person who sleeps late

smockfaced—baby faced

stake and rider—colonial fence made by bracing stakes together in Xs and laying pieces of wood (called riders) across the top

stentorian—very loud; from Stentor, a Greek herald in the Trojan War whose voice was louder than fifty men

tankard—large drinking mug, sometimes with a lid

toadeater—someone who always agrees with his superiors

toddy—a hot spiced drink made of whiskey or brandy

Tory—a loyalist

totty-headed—silly

traces—straps hooking an animal to the vehicle it pulls

trencher—carved wooden platter or bowl
trice—an instant, a moment
tricorne—a hat with three corners
tuppence—a coin worth two pennies
twigged—observed, saw through
vedettes—sentries (guards) on horseback
witcrackers—people who made jokes
witling—a fool
zany—crazy (person)

Further Reading
for Young People

Boorstin, Daniel J. *The Landmark History of the American People.* New York: Random House, 1968.

Clyne, Patricia Edwards. *Patriots in Petticoats.* New York: Dodd, Mead & Co., 1976.

Evans, R. E. *The War of American Independence.* Cambridge Introduction to World History Series. Cambridge, England: Cambridge University Press, 1976.

Hayes, Nancy. "Portraitist of the Revolution: Charles Willson Peale." In *Cobblestone: The History Magazine for Young People,* September 1984, 21–25.

Perl, Lila. *Slumps, Grunts, and Snickerdoodles: What Colonial America Ate and Why.* New York: Clarion-Seabury, 1975.

Sloane, Eric. *A Museum of Early American Tools.* New York: Ballantine Books, 1964.

Tunis, Edwin. *Colonial Living*. New York: Crowell, 1957.

Uncommon Soldier of the Revolution, The: Women and Young People Who Fought for American Independence. Harrisburg, Pa.: Eastern Acorn Press, 1986.

Wilbur, C. Keith. *Picture Book of the Continental Soldier*. Harrisburg, Pa.: Stackpole Books, 1969.

————. *Revolutionary Medicine: 1700–1800*. Chester, Conn.: Globe Pequot Press, 1980.

Selected Bibliography

Bill, Alfred Hoyt. *Valley Forge: The Making of an Army.* New York: Harper and Brothers, 1952.

Busch, Noel F. *Winter Quarters: George Washington and the Continental Army at Valley Forge.* New York: Liveright, 1974.

Calhoun, Robert McCluer. *The Loyalist in Revolutionary America.* New York: Harcourt Brace, 1973.

Fletcher, Stevenson Whitcomb. *Pennsylvania Agriculture and Country Life: 1640–1840.* Harrisburg, Pa.: Pennsylvania Historical and Museum Commission, 1971.

Jackson, John W. *Whitemarsh 1777: Impregnable Stronghold.* Fort Washington, Pa.: Historical Society of Fort Washington, 1984.

———. *With the British Army in Philadelphia 1777–1778.* San Rafael, Calif.: Presidio Press, 1979.

Pancake, John S. *1777: The Year of the Hangman*. University, Ala.: University of Alabama Press, 1977.

Trussell, John B. B., Jr. "The Battle of Brandywine." In *Historic Pennsylvania Leaflet* 37, edited by Donald H. Kent and William A. Hunter. Harrisburg, Pa.: Pennsylvania Historical and Museum Commission, 1974.

————. *Birthplace of an Army: A Study of the Valley Forge Encampment*. Harrisburg, Pa.: Pennsylvania Historical and Museum Commission, 1979.

Well, Peter. *The American War of Independence*. New York: Holmes and Meier Publishers, 1978.

Wright, Esmond, ed. *The Fire of Liberty*. London: The Folio Society, 1983.

Dorothea Jensen is a former teacher of English. After moving to Minnesota from Philadelphia, she wrote *The Riddle of Penncroft Farm* to make the American Revolution come alive for her own children. She lives in southern New Hampshire, in a colonial house built in the 1700s.

Have you read these
Great Episodes?

ANN RINALDI

An Acquaintance with Darkness

*A Break with Charity: A Story about
the Salem Witch Trials*

*Cast Two Shadows:
The American Revolution in the South*

*The Coffin Quilt: The Feud between
the Hatfields and the McCoys*

*The Fifth of March:
A Story of the Boston Massacre*

*Finishing Becca: A Story about
Peggy Shippen and Benedict Arnold*

*Hang a Thousand Trees with Ribbons:
The Story of Phillis Wheatley*

*A Ride into Morning:
The Story of Tempe Wick*

The Secret of Sarah Revere

The Staircase

ROLAND SMITH

*The Captain's Dog: My Journey with
the Lewis and Clark Tribe*

THEODORE TAYLOR

*Air Raid—Pearl Harbor!
The Story of December 7, 1941*